NOTHING EVI

Why, why, did everything have to change?

For Sandie it meant a whole new life – with the mother she'd hardly seen since she was a small child. It wasn't just that they didn't get on: Sandie's mother hated music – the one thing Sandie loved most in the world, the talent she had inherited from her father. It looked like the end of all her ambitions . . .

Peggy Burns has written a number of books for children, including *Killer Dog*, *Secret of the Driftwood Elephant* and *River in Flood*, all published by Lion Publishing. This is her first book for teenagers.

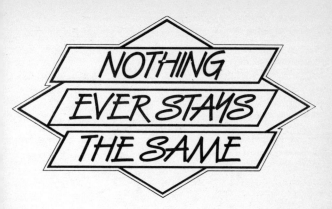

NOTHING EVER STAYS THE SAME

PEGGY BURNS

A LION PAPERBACK

Tring • Batavia • Sydney

Copyright © 1987 Peggy Burns

Published by
Lion Publishing plc
Icknield Way, Tring, Herts, England
ISBN 0 7459 1249 4
Albatross Books Pty Ltd
PO Box 320, Sutherland, NSW 2232, Australia
ISBN 0 86760 882 X

First edition 1987

British Library Cataloguing in Publication Data
Burns, Peggy
  Nothing ever stays the same.
  I. Title
  823'.914 [F]   PZ7
  ISBN 0-7459-1249-4

Printed and bound in Great Britain
by Cox & Wyman Ltd, Reading

CHAPTER ONE

To begin with, the Dreadful Day was just the same as any other day. Washing, dressing, piano practice. The postman dropped a bill through the letter-box, and Gramps said a bad word. The toast burnt itself as usual the second I took my eyes off it, and Gran said, 'Never mind, love,' like she always did. I made tea for them in the big brown pot, and a cup of coffee for myself. Gramps sat at the breakfast table and propped his morning paper against the milk-jug. Nothing was any different.

And then, without any warning, my gran dropped the cup of tea she was passing across the table to Gramps. I stared like an idiot at the broken bits of china and the brown puddle spreading across the white cloth. Then I snatched up the first thing I saw and found I was mopping at the sodden tablecloth with Gran's clean apron.

I piled all the broken bits together.

Gran was rubbing her arm. I watched her. 'I must be getting old,' she said. 'Can't even give someone a cup of tea without spilling it!'

But it was more than that. Gran looked sick . . . positively green. She looked like Ricky Pinardi looked when he fell off the bike-shed roof and broke his arm. I said, 'Are you sure you're OK, Gran? You look a bit pale. I think I'd better not go to school today — I'll stay at home in case you need me.'

'Indeed you won't!' She sounded cross, but I knew she wasn't. 'Don't fuss, child — you're worse than an old woman!'

Gramps winked at me over the top of his paper. He really thought I was trying it on. 'Better luck next time!' he said. He didn't seem to have noticed the way she looked.

But there *was* something wrong, and I knew it. Gran hadn't just spilled that tea, she'd dropped the cup and saucer. Simply let go of it — and that wasn't like Gran at all.

It was an awful day. I kept telling myself that there was nothing to worry about. So she dropped a cup. Big deal. Everyone has accidents.

But somehow I couldn't forget it. It nagged at my mind all day long. For the first time ever Sharon Blake got more than me in a maths test. And when I couldn't spell 'photosynthesis' old Coley made me write it out thirty times. And he said a lot of sarcastic stuff about what was between my ears. That was the only thing I learned that day — how to spell 'photosynthesis'. Apart from that, school was a complete waste of time. After about a hundred years, the bell went at three-thirty.

I ran all the way home. Past the shops, and the 'Dog and Duck', and the old chapel, where Mr Shaw, the caretaker, was standing on a step-ladder and sticking another of their corny posters on the notice-board. I didn't stop to read it.

I knew as soon as I opened the door that something awful had happened. Mrs Fisher from next door was with Gramps — sitting in Gran's

6

chair. What was *she* doing here? And where was Gran? I knew there was something wrong, I'd known all day . . . My mouth was suddenly dry, and the palms of my hands went all tickly and sweaty.

I said, 'Where is she?'

'Now, dearie, don't take on so,' Mrs Fisher said in a kind voice. 'Your gran had a nasty turn. She was . . .'

'She isn't . . .' I had to force the words past the lump that suddenly seemed to have grown in my throat. 'She's not . . . dead?'

'Dead?' Gramps' pale old eyes opened wide. 'Nay, lass,' he said in his slow Yorkshire voice, 'it'll take more than a funny turn to kill your gran. She's been taken to hospital, though, right enough.'

I sat down then. My legs had gone all wobbly and funny.

Gramps himself seemed suddenly old. Old and shrivelled and pathetic, his face wrinkled like an ancient walnut. Only his voice was cheerful, trying hard to hide his own misery.

'What's the matter with her?' I had to ask – though I was afraid to hear the answer.

'A stroke, the doctor thinks,' Mrs Fisher put in, her false teeth clacking, as they always did. I wished she would go away. I wanted to know what a stroke was, but I didn't want to ask while Mrs Fisher was here. Just me and Gramps would be easier.

'When will she be able to come home?' I was looking at Gramps, but it was Mrs Fisher who answered me again.

'Well now – we must look on the bright side,

mustn't we?' She talked in a brisk, jolly-along voice, the teeth clacking all the time. 'It might not be for very long — six or eight weeks, perhaps.'

'But that's two whole months!'

'It seems a long time just now — but the weeks will soon pass by — you'll see. And I know you're going to be a brave and sensible girl . . .'

She talks to me as if I were a little kid, I thought angrily.

I looked at Gramps, and our eyes met. His old hands, thin and mottled with brown splotches, trembled on the arms of the chair. How would the two of us manage without Gran? I couldn't imagine what life would be like without her. She'd always been there, strong and dependable. I suppose we'd get along somehow, but it wasn't going to be easy. And how would we get to visit her? The General Hospital was miles away and we didn't have a car.

As if she knew what I was thinking, Mrs Fisher said briskly, 'I've been doing some telephoning this afternoon, dearie, and I've made arrangements for your grandfather to stay with his sister until your gran comes home. That means he'll be nearer the hospital for visiting. It's all fixed up. I thought that . . .'

'He doesn't need to go to his sister's,' I chipped in. I couldn't help myself. 'I can look after him. We'll look after each other — we'll be all right together, won't we, Gramps? I can do the cooking, and the cleaning . . .'

Mrs Fisher laughed suddenly.

It was the kind of laugh that makes you feel you've said something incredibly stupid. I could feel myself blushing, and the more I tried not to, the hotter my cheeks got. It was horrible.

'Don't be ridiculous, Sandie,' the woman went on, 'a child like you! Why − you need looking after yourself! Now, I've arranged for him to . . .'

'You've arranged!'

Who did she think she was? Sticking her long nose in where it wasn't wanted. I knew I was going to be rude, and I didn't even want to stop myself.

'Who gave you the right to come around here and arrange our lives!' I shouted. 'Why don't you just go away and mind your own business?'

'Well!' gasped Mrs Fisher. She stood with her mouth open, as if turned to stone.

'Sandie, don't. Don't talk like that, love − Mrs Fisher's been kind. She only wants to help.' Gramps' voice was thin and reedy and somehow far away.

'We don't need help. We can manage quite well on our own, thank you, Mrs Fisher,' I said, stonily.

'Well!' the woman repeated. 'I've never been spoken to like that in all my life! I hope that's not the way you'll speak to your mother!'

'My mother!' I said sharply. 'What's *she* got to do with it?'

'Your mother will be here in the morning to take you back with her for a few weeks,' Mrs Fisher said. 'Now, don't look like that, Sandie − you know as well as I do that you and your grandfather couldn't possibly stay here alone. Your mother is the obvious person to take care of you − she herself thinks it's a good idea. She's going to have a word with the Head at the local school about you going there for a while. She told me on the phone that she's thought a lot recently about sending for you.

She has her own fashion shop now, you know – she *could* have you with her all the time if she wanted to. And, goodness knows, your poor gran and grandad need the rest! Of course, it will be a nice change for you, too!'

With every word she said I could feel the tight lump of misery in my chest turning slowly to ice. But my face was still burning, as if it was on fire.

All these years, I thought. The years I've spent with Gran and Gramps because she and Dad split up. All that time, she never wanted me – she was too busy living her own life. Always too busy to care. Why should she want me now?

I said, gruffly, 'I haven't seen her for a year. If I *have* to go away somewhere, I'd rather stay with Dad at his flat.'

There was a funny look on Mrs Fisher's face. Like she knew something she didn't want me to know.

'We rang to let him know, of course, and he's arranging to come up for a few days to be with his mother. I did ask him about your staying with him until she's better – I know you've spent quite a lot of time with him. But I'm afraid it's not convenient for him to have you there just now.'

Not convenient. It never had been convenient. It wasn't convenient for them to have a daughter at all. Why had they ever bothered? Why was I even alive?

But they must have been a family once, long ago, before all the quarrelling and shouting. There must have been a time when they loved each other, and me. And suddenly the one, brief memory came back, a bit like a happy dream, only much more vivid – I hadn't thought of it for a long time.

I was a very little girl. I was wearing a pink dress – I could even see that – pink, with pale blue flowers. I'd hurt myself in some way, and I was crying. I saw myself being lifted on to my mother's knee and cuddled close.

And near by was the piano, with Dad playing and smiling across at us both – it seemed impossible, somehow, to think of my father *not* playing a piano – perhaps that was why I loved music so much. But in the memory, I even knew the name of the tune – 'The Dream of Olwen' – it had been my favourite. In those days, things must have been all right between Mother and Dad.

But something had happened to make them not love each other any more. To make them want to give me away to Gran and Gramps.

It was like 'pass the parcel', I thought – with me as the parcel.

The old clock on the mantelpiece downstairs dinged slowly three times.

I sighed and turned over yet again. Three o'clock in the morning, but my brain was too busy to sleep. How *could* I sleep? My whole life was ending . . .

I knew now what a 'stroke' was, and I was picturing poor Gran in her white hospital bed, helpless, paralysed down one side. What was happening to her right now, at this very minute? Was she asleep or was she like me, lying awake and being tormented by thoughts that wouldn't let her rest? How long would it be before Gran was back to normal? *Would she ever be?*

I shut my eyes tightly, thrusting the terrible

thought away with all my strength. They sprung open again, as if the lids were on wires. Of course Gran would get well – she *had* to! Because, if she didn't, I'd have to stay with my mother – and how could I bear more than a few weeks there?

'She doesn't like me, and I don't like her.' I said the words aloud.

I knew it was true. My mother never *had* liked me, though she *acted* as though she did. I sometimes stayed with her in the school holidays, and I'd spent Christmas there once. She'd taken me to see *Superman*, and we'd been swimming at the Leisure Centre. At least, I swam and she sat at a little table and watched. I'd even had riding lessons. And that Christmas she had given me an enormous doll's house with an elevator on the side and a roof-top swimming pool. But all the time I could tell that she didn't like me.

Now, quite suddenly, I could see the reason for it. It was like being in a car in the rain, when you can't see out of the window, and somebody suddenly turns on the screen wipers.

'I'm too much like my father,' I said in surprise. I'd never thought of it before.

That was it. That was the reason my mother had no piano in the house, the reason she hated to hear me play, even on the guitar.

'She hates him – and she hates me because I'm like him!' I whispered into my pillow.

And how could I bear living with someone who hated me?

I remembered that Mrs Fisher had said that Gran and Gramps needed a rest. What if, even when Gran was better, I still couldn't come home?

What if I had to stay there *for ever*?

12

CHAPTER TWO

My case stood ready packed by the door, the end of my white belt snaking out from under the lid. My mother would say I was untidy, but that was nothing new. In a plastic carrier-bag were my roller-boots and a big bundle of music. My guitar, in its case, leaned against the wall. She couldn't stand me playing it, but I wasn't going to leave it behind.

Gramps and I had tried to eat breakfast – cornflakes and over-done toast as usual, both of us putting on an act, pretending that nothing had changed. Was it really only yesterday, at breakfast, that Gran had dropped that cup? Miserably, I put down my piece of toast. Another mouthful would choke me.

There were so many important things to say, but neither of us was saying them. Instead we talked about silly things like letting the milkman know that the house would be empty, and cancelling the newspapers, and about asking Mrs Fisher to come in to water the geraniums.

And then, suddenly, there was no time to talk about the things that really mattered, like Gran getting well, and about sending for me the very minute Gramps got back from his sister's. My mother's Volkswagen pulled up outside the gate, and I heard the quick clacking of her high heels on the garden path. The doorbell rang.

'You'll let me know, Gramps?' I said, desperately. 'About Gran? You'll phone me tomorrow?'

Gramps put out his hand and stroked my hair. He doesn't do that very often. He said, 'Aye, lass.' That was all, but we understood each other.

The bell sounded again, twice, impatiently. I got up to open the door.

'Well, Mr Harland, it's good to see you again – though I wish the circumstances were happier! And Sandra – how you've grown!'

She'd be more surprised if I hadn't grown at all, I thought, ready to take offence at anything she said. And calling me 'Sandra'. I hadn't been called that since I was five years old. She did it every time. 'She's only just walked through the door,' I said to myself, 'and she's getting to me already.'

I said, 'Hello, Mother.'

She looked me up and down, frowning. 'Have you nothing better to wear than a tattered pair of jeans and a baggy sweater?' she asked. 'And your hair . . . don't you possess a comb? Really, Sandra, I would have thought that you would have developed some pride in your appearance at your age. I have to call in and see a collection this morning – that's why I had to come so early. I was away by six. But I can't take you to a Fashion House looking like Huckleberry Finn.'

'I've got my white dress, but it's packed,' I said.

'It'll soon unpack again. Run up quick and change,' Gramps suggested.

'No, never mind. We'll stop on the motorway for

a coffee. You can change in the Ladies.' She picked up my case. 'Is this all you're bringing?' she asked in surprise. 'You'll need all your clothes, you know – you'll be with me for quite some time.'

'I've got all I'll need,' I said gruffly. 'There's no point in bringing my winter things.'

'If she needs anything else I'll have it sent on,' said Gramps hastily.

I gave him a quick kiss on his cheek, and whispered in his ear, 'You won't forget?' He squeezed my shoulder, and I knew he wouldn't.

'Look after yourself, Gramps.'

'Come along, Sandra – we really must be off. So nice to have seen you again, Mr Harland. I hope you'll have good news of your wife soon.'

He's her father-in-law, I realized in surprise. But she was talking to him as if he were a complete stranger.

Gramps came to the gate with us and watched as my mother stowed my stuff away in the boot. But as we drove away, I didn't look back. I knew he'd be smiling, trying to look cheerful for my sake, and I couldn't pretend any more that I wasn't feeling miserable. I saw Mrs Fisher's curtains twitch as we passed her house. Old Nosy Parker. I turned my head away, and caught a glimpse of the new poster outside the chapel. It said, 'The family that prays together, stays together'. How corny could you get? What families were ever like that?

We drove in silence for a long time. Neither of us knew what to talk about. At last I said, 'Can I put some music on?' She had a cassette-player under the dashboard, but I couldn't see any tapes for it.

'Help yourself,' my mother said. 'The tapes are in the glove compartment. I've no noisy rock music, though. Or Mozart, either. That's what you like, isn't it? Weird choice of music. Middle-of-the-road stuff is all I've got.'

Very middle-of-the-road, I thought, sorting through the cassettes. But anything was better than that awful silence.

Things got a bit better after we stopped at the motorway services. The white dress was a bit crumpled but it improved my appearance, and my mother bought two pale blue combs to keep my hair out of my eyes.

She gave a quick nod. 'That's much better. But I really must get you some new clothes. And your hair needs styling. It's like driving around with Primitive Man.'

That was where she and I were so different. I wasn't really bothered about what I looked like. I lived in jeans and a tee-shirt when I wasn't at school. And I hated having my hair done. Lisa, my friend, called me an untidy slob, but I didn't care. But my mother . . . I looked across at her as she changed into top gear, slid the car back into the fast motorway traffic and headed across the Pennines towards Thornbridge. She looked exactly what she was – a successful business woman. Stylish black two-piece suit, red silk blouse. Nice make-up, not too much of it. I thought, 'She's not bad looking for thirty-seven.' She still had a nice figure, and her hair was still dark and shiny. I wondered if she dyed it. Lisa's mother's hair was going grey and she was only thirty. She had been a teenage bride, Lisa had told me; she and her dad had run away together, all lovey-dovey and romantic. But now they had four kids, and fought all the time. It seemed to me like love was never meant to last – though it had with Gran and Gramps. Perhaps they were just different?

The Fashion House, when we got there, was just as boring as I expected. It was a nice place but there was nothing to do. I sat in a deep chair in a fancy waiting-room full of plants in big tubs and looked at some glossy fashion magazines and drank real coffee with too much sugar in it. My mother was a very long time, but when at last she did re-appear, she was smiling and relaxed.

'Sorry I've been so long, darling,' she said. 'But now that business is over with we can go on and have lunch somewhere. What would you like to do this afternoon?'

'Could we just go home, please?' I said.

'But of course that's what you'll want to do. I wasn't thinking. You'll want to unpack your things. And you're wondering about your poor gran, too, I know. We'll ring the hospital when we get in. I'm sure she's going to be all right though, Sandra – you mustn't worry so much!'

I took a deep breath. 'Mother – couldn't you call me Sandie? It's what everyone calls me.'

My mother frowned. 'I don't like nicknames,' she said. 'And Sandra is the name you were given.' She looked up at me and smiled suddenly. 'But I suppose I could try,' she added.

Well, that was better than nothing. And whatever she called me, it couldn't really matter much. Because it was only going to be for a few weeks. We rang the hospital. 'No change,' they told us.

I changed back into my jeans and hung up the white dress and my school clothes in the wardrobe. Everything else I stuffed into a drawer. There was nothing else to do. I flopped down on my back on the bed and looked around.

The room was nice. It had been decorated since the last time I was here. There were fitted wardrobes along the walls with mirrors in the front, and a pink carpet that your feet sank into. There was a bedside lamp with a deep pink frilly shade to match the one that hung from the ceiling. Everything else was a creamy white, even the quilt cover on the bed. It was all modern and expensive and beautiful, like everything else in the house. But I wondered if it would ever feel like home. It certainly wasn't like Gran's, where my walls were covered in posters almost to the ceiling, and socks hung out of drawers, and games that never got put away were piled on top of the chest. And Theodore, my giant teddy, sat in his corner, wearing an old cap of Gramps' with yellow stuffing seeping out of a hole in his tummy. Suddenly, I wished I'd brought him with me. Just remembering him made me home-sick.

I sat up and blew my nose, and swallowed the lump in my throat. What a wimp I was! Homesick, and I'd only been there an hour!

I took my guitar out of its case, and my fingers struck a few angry chords, then began to wander across the strings, picking out a melody that seemed to come from inside me. At first it was a hard, bitter sound, like the way I'd felt about Gran being ill, and then with Mrs Nosy Fisher from next door. But gradually the music changed – now a soft minor key was taking over, and all the sadness and heartache and longing were flowing into the music, and I was playing with tears running down my cheeks and dripping on to my sweater.

And then a pebble hit the window with a sudden sharp click.

I put my guitar down quickly, dug in my pocket for a tissue and mopped my face. What a wally – crying like that – pouring myself into the music. And with someone listening, too. Another pebble, bigger than the last, missed the glass and came sailing into the room through the open side-window. I picked it up and stuck my head out.

My bedroom was at the back of the house. Beyond our garden was the back of a terrace of old houses, every one the same, with a sticking-out kitchen built on. A boy about my age, with ginger hair and a faceful of freckles, was standing on the other side of our fence, his arm raised to fling another stone. He saw me, and his arm dropped to his side.

'I wanted to see who was playing,' he shouted across to me.

'So now you know. Do you want a photograph?' I yelled back. I was hopping mad, with myself as much as with him.

'There's no need to be like that,' he shouted.

I grabbed the window catch and yanked at it. It stuck fast, and I saw I had to undo the bar at the bottom too.

'Hey!' the boy yelled. 'It was great!'

The window shut with a crash, and I drew the curtains too.

How come everybody in the whole world was a Nosy Parker?

CHAPTER THREE

The next day started all wrong. It was my own fault
– I should have known better.

I asked my mother about music lessons.

My fingers were itching for a piano, and I didn't
know where to find one. I knew she could afford to
hire one while I was there, or *buy* one, even. I
thought she might have changed her mind about
hearing me play. How wrong can you be?

She was just slotting slices of bread into the
toaster (pale gold toast instead of dark brown was
a nice change). As soon as I had the words out she
rammed the switch down so hard that she broke a
French Pink fingernail.

'Sandie – we've had all this out before.' Her
voice was low and even. I knew she was trying not
to lose her temper, and even then I couldn't leave
the subject alone.

'I haven't mentioned it for ages,' I persisted.
'And I don't see why I shouldn't have music
lessons. I have them at home. My fingers'll get stiff
if I don't practise.'

'I said no, and I mean no,' said my mother. 'So
sit down and drink your coffee. I don't want to hear
any more about it.'

'But, Mother . . .'

Her voice rose. 'That's the *end* of it!'

I sat viciously stirring sugar into my cup. It really wasn't fair. I could see exactly what she was trying to do. If she could, she'd crush every bit of the music out of me, and turn me into somebody like herself. All that talk about clothes and hairstyles and stuff. All I wanted was just to be *me*.

'All this is because *he's* a musician, isn't it?' I said. 'You can't bear the thought that I might turn out to be like my dad.'

'Sandie – that's *enough*!'

But I went on. 'You can't even bear to hear me talk about him, can you? Just what did he do that was so awful?'

She caught her breath then, and when I saw the way she looked I wished I hadn't said that. There was silence.

She took the butter out of the fridge and began spreading it on the toast, slap, slap, slap. After a bit she said, 'What can a child like you possibly know about it?'

I didn't say anything, and she began talking again. 'I can't imagine what your grandparents are thinking of, allowing you to grow up with such atrocious manners. I don't like the way you speak to me, young lady, and the sooner you change it, the better you and I will get along.' She sighed then. 'Perhaps it's partly my own fault – I would have had you with me when you were small, but I wanted to build my career first, and get a nice home together for us. I can see now that I was wrong.'

We ate toast in silence. I didn't like that dig about my grandparents. My bad manners were nothing to do with them. I couldn't remember being rude to people before – at least, not very often. Just this last couple of days, and then I couldn't help it.

To change the subject, I said, 'Who's the boy who lives in the end house over the back? A boy with freckles and red hair?'

My mother drained her coffee cup and began to collect the washing up together. 'You must mean Jonathan Miles,' she said. 'Where have you seen him?'

'He was in his garden yesterday. I was looking out of my bedroom window.'

'Get to know him if you like – I suppose you need people your own age. But don't get too friendly with him.'

'I don't fancy him, if that's what you mean.'

'Don't be silly. It's just that they're a bit strange. At least, their neighbours say so. They have people in the house for religious meetings, and *sing* – something to do with the church up the road. Mrs Ellis next door went there with them once, and she says it's not like any church she's been in before. It's all clapping and singing and people hugging each other. She didn't mind it – she says it's nice and lively, and friendly. But it wouldn't do for me. Imagine – *clapping* in church! It doesn't seem right, somehow.'

They sounded slightly potty. That boy looked all right – but you never could tell. He might be a real Holy Joe, I thought, swallowing my last piece of toast.

'Just stack those things in the dishwasher, will you, Sandie – I have to get down to the shop. Come with me if you like, and we'll have a look for something nice in your size. And later on we'll call

22

in at the school and see the Head about you starting there. There's no telling how long your gran's going to be out of action.'

I said I'd rather stay at home. I couldn't imagine anything worse than spending an afternoon looking at dresses. My mother shrugged her shoulders. 'It will be a long day,' she said, glancing at her watch, 'but I suppose you know best. Put a film on the video if you like. The tapes are in the cupboard.'

She was right. It was a long day. I played the guitar a bit, and watched little kids' programmes on the telly – I didn't know how to work the video, so I didn't bother with it. Gran didn't have one. She didn't have a dishwasher either. She used to say, 'Why pay out all that money – I've got a dishwasher already.' She meant me.

Halfway through the morning Holy Joe's mother came out and hung about three hundred nappies on the clothes line. And soon after that she began to play the piano. It must have been her, because I didn't see anyone else around, and Holy Joe Jonathan would be in school. She didn't play very well, and I didn't know the tune. But it was a piano – and it was in tune, too.

It was a sunny day, so after lunch I settled down in a garden chair on the lawn, a pile of magazines by my side. I hadn't slept well last night, so before long my eyes grew heavy and I nodded right off to sleep. Some time later a voice jerked me awake.

'Well, well, if it isn't old "Fiddler on the roof".'

I must have been asleep for ages – the sun had moved round. I was sitting in the shade, and I was cold. The red-haired boy was sitting on the fence, grinning at me.

I suppose I was glad, really. After the way I'd shouted at him yesterday, he might never have spoken to me again. And I wanted to get near that piano.

I said, 'It's you again' – and then couldn't think of anything else to say.

He probably felt as shy as I did, because there was an uncomfortable silence. After a minute he cleared his throat and said, 'I wasn't being nosy yesterday, about your guitar-playing, and all that. It's just that I'm learning the guitar, too – but I'm nothing like as good as you are. I wish I could play like that – all those fantastic chords!'

'How long have you been learning?' I asked him.

'About a year,' he said. 'Our youth leader at church is teaching me.'

He was starting already. Going on about his church. Was he really a religious nut? Or did he only go there because he *had* to?

I said, 'You poor thing. Your parents make you go every Sunday, and all that?'

'I don't mind.'

'Well, I would. All that boring hymn singing . . . My gran used to make me go with her sometimes. Harvest Festivals and Sunday school anniversaries – little kids spouting a lot of potty rhymes. All pie-in-the-sky stuff. Nothing to do with real life.'

He said, 'That's not the way Jesus meant it to be.'

I groaned. 'Do we have to talk about Jesus?'

'Well, you started this conversation.'

'And I'm changing it. Let's talk about something else. Who else is in your family? Have you got any sisters?'

24

He shook his head. 'Only Splodge.'

'Is that the dog?'

He laughed. 'That's the baby. My brother.'

'That's not really his name, is it?'

'His name's Roger.'

'Then why's he called Splodge? Poor kid.'

'Wait till you see the way he eats.' The boy slid off the fence into our garden and walked towards me across the grass. 'I haven't seen you around here before,' he said. 'Is the fashion lady your aunt? Are you visiting her, or what?'

I looked away from him. 'She's my mother,' I said quietly. 'I live with my grandparents, but my gran had a stroke . . . I don't know how long I'll have to stay here.'

'Don't you want to stay?'

I looked away again. 'We don't get on, me and my mother . . . You ask a lot of questions, don't you?'

'So do you. But I won't ask any more if you don't want me to. How can you get to know someone without asking questions, though? Say, "Please tell me about your life"?'

I grinned at him. It did sound a bit ridiculous.

'Asking questions doesn't mean you're being nosy,' he said. 'It just shows that you're interested. And I'm interested in playing the guitar. So my next question – if I was allowed to ask one – would be, "How long have you been playing?" After all, you asked me the same thing. But, if you'd rather not . . .'

I laughed and said, 'Don't be an idiot. I don't mind, really. My father bought me a small size guitar when I was a little kid. I've been playing ever since my fingers were long enough to reach across the strings.'

'Your father? I didn't know you had one.'

That was a polite way of asking a question without really asking one, if you see what I mean. But now I'd got talking to him I realized I really *didn't* mind. There's this girl at our school, Sally Coates; she talks all the time. You can tell she's not interested in anything *you* have to say. She's thinking all the time of what she's going to say next. Jonathan asked a lot of questions, but he was good at listening as well. I'd only known him for half an hour but I found myself telling him about my mother and dad being divorced, and about Gran being ill in hospital. I even told him how much I missed playing the piano, and how my mother wouldn't let me go on with my lessons.

He said, 'We've got a piano. You could come over and play ours.'

He couldn't have known that that's just what I was hoping he'd say.

CHAPTER FOUR

When my mother came home from the shop she was carrying a couple of dresses in plastic covers and several bags which said 'Eloise, Fashions' on the side (her name was Louise but Eloise sounds more elegant for a dress shop).

We had wholewheat lasagne and salad for supper – she lived on that kind of stuff, because of her figure – then she started fishing clothes out of the bags. For the first time in my life I was sorry I wasn't interested in fashion. Because if I had been, I'd have gone wild over them. I tried on skirts and tops, shirts and dresses, while my mother walked around me criticizing everything.

'No, no, that collar is too big, you look as if you're about to take off . . . That one's a possibility, it's just your shade of pink . . . Oh, no – that's ghastly, take it off again . . .'

She had just about narrowed the choice down to three skirts, two blouses and a dress, when the doorbell rang.

My mother glanced at her watch. 'Goodness – that'll be Bill,' she said. 'He's earlier than usual.'

She didn't say who Bill was, but he kissed her on the cheek when he came in, and she introduced him as 'a friend of mine'.

If he was her boyfriend, I didn't think much of

him. He was old – he must have been at least forty – and he wasn't even good-looking. He wasn't much taller than her, and he wore glasses and was going bald on top – some strands of hair were brushed across to hide the bald bit.

'Hi there,' he said to me jovially. 'Glad to have a chance to get to know you at last. I've heard a lot about you. Starting school soon, are you?'

'On Monday,' my mother said. 'I forgot to tell you, Sandie.'

'Ah,' Bill said. 'You're going to love that, aren't you? Tell me, what do you like best at school? English? Arithmetic?'

I decided straight away that I didn't like him. He was talking *at* me all the time, as if he didn't think of me as a real person. But it wasn't what he said so much as the way he looked when he said it. He looked at my forehead, my chin, the wall behind me – anywhere but my eyes. No, I didn't like him.

'When I was your age,' he went on, 'the thing I liked best about school was the holidays! But I bet you're good at your lessons, aren't you?'

I looked straight at him. 'Yes,' I said firmly. 'I'm good at music, *just like my father*.'

My mother gasped. 'Sandie!'

Bill said coldly, 'Hey – we're not in some kind of competition, you know. He went off and left her a long time ago.'

I could have slapped his pink piggy face. Where had he got that idea from? Knowing my mother, I'd say it was more likely that *she'd* gone off and left Dad!

Nobody had told me much about the way they'd split up – if I ever asked Gran she always said,

'Least said, soonest mended.' She told me that my mother couldn't stand being left on her own night after night while he went out with his band – he played the piano at the Starlight Club. He's still got that job now, and the long hours *are* a pain. When I was younger it was worse, because whenever I went to stay with him old Mrs Greenwood from the next flat had to come over and sit with me until he came home. I couldn't believe he had left my mother – it had to be the other way around. My dad was kind and jolly and full of fun. He wouldn't have done anything like that.

So I went off to my room. I was hopping mad, and I didn't care if Bill knew it.

Later on they went out to the pub. I went to bed but I heard his car come back about eleven o'clock. I slipped out on to the landing in the dark as the front door opened, and the two of them came in together. I really hadn't meant to spy on them – I don't know what I went out there for, but when he took her in his arms I stood as if I'd grown roots. And as he kissed her, I gripped the banister rail till I could see the white bumps of my knuckles. I turned away feeling sicker than I'd ever felt in my life.

I don't know why I felt like that. After all, she and Dad weren't married any more. What could it matter? But it seemed to me as if they *should* be still together. We ought to be a family – me and Mother and Dad.

All of a sudden it seemed as if the grown-up world was just too complicated.

I got a telling-off the next day.

I couldn't see that what I had done was so terrible, and I told her so.

'Sandra,' she said (we were back to that now, were we?), 'as long as you are under my roof I insist that you are polite to my guests.'

'Guest? Huh — that's one way to describe him I suppose. And what did I say to him, anyway? Only that I was good at music like my dad. It's perfectly true.'

'You know very well what I mean. It was the way you said it. And mentioning your father like that to Bill! That marriage was over and done with years ago, and I won't have that man dragged into conversation with my friends.'

' "That man" was your husband! You got married in church in a white dress and a veil — I've seen Gran's photos! You must have loved him, or you would never have married him in the first place. You lived with him for eight years. Eight years! Doesn't that mean anything to you? Haven't you got any feelings?'

My mother's face was as white as the plaster wall.

'I have got feelings. And you are trampling on them with every word you say,' she declared. She was trembling. 'Just remember, I want you to be polite when Bill is here. I was ashamed of you last night.'

'Hmph. You were ashamed of *me*? That's a laugh. How do you think I felt about you,' I said, hating her, 'kissing and cuddling in the hallway like a . . . like a couple of teenagers. At your age!' I shuddered. 'How can you bear to let him kiss you like that? He's awful.'

My mother spoke quietly. 'He has asked me to marry him.'

'Marry him? Mother! You wouldn't marry that creep?'

'He may not be your idea of Mr Universe. But Sandie — it's not what people look like on the outside . . . you're old enough to know that. He's a very special person.'

'So you said "yes"?'

She nodded. 'I said "yes". We're getting married in November. I was hoping that you and Bill would get on well, and that maybe we could all make a fresh start together. At your age a girl needs a mother — it's not right that you should be growing up with old people.'

I was horrified. 'Make a fresh start together? You and me and Bill? What about Gran and Gramps?'

I shook my head. What had I got to do with my mother and her boyfriend? I'd managed without them for years. Gran and Gramps were my family — and with them I had my music too. How long would it be before I could go back home?

'Sandie,' my mother said, breaking into my thoughts, 'you're not giving me a fair chance. Or Bill either. He's nice when you get to know him.'

'I don't want to get to know him,' I shouted. 'I don't want anything to do with him. Why can't you see that I just don't belong here?'

I went out of the house and slammed the door after me. She followed me out and shouted, 'Sandie — don't be so childish!'

I yelled back, 'I *am* a child — you tell me so often enough!'

Without thinking, I marched down the garden, climbed over the fence and knocked on Jonathan's back door.

It opened straight away – perhaps it was as well, as I might have changed my mind and gone away again – and Jonathan's mother stood there with a baby on one arm and a pile of nappies under the other. She smiled at me.

'You must be Sandie Harland,' she said. 'Jonathan's told me about you. Come on in.'

Feeling tongue-tied, I followed her into the house.

'Sit down, Sandie,' she said, 'and I'll tell Jonathan you're here. Just hold Splodge a minute, will you?' And I found myself sitting on a chair with the baby on my knee. What did I say to it? How did I hold it? I joggled my knees up and down, and the baby looked up at me and chuckled.

'He likes you,' his mother said, coming back into the room followed by Jonathan. 'You must have a knack with babies.'

'I've never held one before,' I told her. 'He's nice.'

'Of course he's nice. He takes after his big brother,' Jonathan said, swinging him off my knee and throwing him up in the air. He caught him expertly on the way down. The baby squealed and giggled, and Jonathan threw him up again.

'He's just had his breakfast – you'll make him sick again,' warned his mother.

'It wasn't my fault he was sick that time,' Jonathan told her. 'It's that yukky stuff you give him to eat.'

But he plonked the baby down in the middle of the floor. Like lightning Splodge made a beeline for a big ginger cat, fast asleep on the floor in a shaft of sunlight. He shuffled across the room on his bottom like a pudgy crab.

'Watch out!' Jonathan shouted.

But before we could stop him, he grabbed a handful of fur and tugged hard. The cat took off like a flea in a fit.

'That poor animal will have a nervous breakdown before long. Splodge treats him like a big furry toy,' sighed Mrs Miles. 'Naughty boy, Splodge! Poor pussy – you mustn't pull his fur like that!' she said to him, and the baby chuckled at her and bounced up and down.

Grinning widely, Jonathan turned to me. 'I was messing about on the computer,' he said. 'Do you want to come and have a game?'

I hesitated, and Mrs Miles said quickly, 'I've got a better idea. You told me that Sandie plays the piano, Jonathan. Do you think you could persuade her to give us a tune?'

I smiled across at her. She knew full well that I wouldn't need much persuading.

CHAPTER FIVE

After that, I took to going over to Jonathan's most days, after school. At first I went because of the piano, but before long I was going because I liked them all. There was always something happening—music and talking and laughing, and Splodge forever in mischief, and silly jokes flying back and forth.

Jonathan's dad was a bus driver. He had a bald head and a beard (Jonathan used to say his hair had slipped), and he told the worst jokes I've ever heard.

'What did William Tell's son say when his father shot the apple off his head?' he'd say.

I'd grin and say, 'I don't know,' and Jonathan would groan.

'That was a narrow escape!' And Mr Miles would prod me in case I'd missed the point. 'An *arrow* escape!'

'Dad – you've told that one a million times!' Jonathan would say. But it never put him off.

My mother seemed to have forgotten that she'd warned me about them, because she never said anything else about me not going over there. And Jonathan came to our house sometimes, too. Anyway, I thought she must have been mistaken about the religious bit, because they never tried to convert me, or anything.

They did have a few Bibles scattered about the

house, and a Christian song book on the piano. And the poster on the kitchen wall, of course. I really liked that poster, and I said so. There was a picture of a hen with chickens underneath its wings – you could see their fluffy yellow faces peeping out – and underneath it said, 'He will cover me with his wings; I will be safe in his care'. It was talking about God, I supposed, but I still liked it.

I told Jonathan about the posters they used to put up outside the chapel on our road. 'A different one every few weeks,' I said. 'You should have seen them. Stuff like "Pray before you stray", and "Anger is only one letter short of danger".' I suddenly remembered the last one: 'The family that prays together, stays together'.

'Does your family pray together?' I asked him.

He blushed, and then nodded. 'Most days we do,' he said. 'Why?'

'Oh, nothing.' But I was thinking that perhaps some of the slogans weren't as corny as they looked, when you really thought about them. This one with the chickens, for instance. It would be nice to feel as safe as that. Like Jonathan and Splodge with their dad. I watched them, with a sudden, peculiar stab of jealousy. Mr Miles always seemed to make time to do things with them – the sort of thing *my* dad had never had the chance to do.

Right now Mr Miles had the baby on his knee, playing 'This is the way the farmer rides'. Every so often they went 'down into the ditch' and while Splodge was on the floor Jonathan would tickle him under his arms, and the baby would have hysterics. Then they did 'This little piggy went to market' and 'Round and round the garden'.

While Mrs Miles got Splodge ready for bed, their dad told us all about what had happened on his bus that day. He always had some funny story or other to tell us. I used to think that driving a bus must be deadly dull – but not any more. You wouldn't believe some of the things he told us.

Mr Miles had been driving the Ivy Green school special. It's a job nobody wants, because the kids are so awful. The bus route goes past this take-away where the owner was in court a year or so back for putting dog-food in his burgers. There's a bus-stop right outside his door, and every day the kids open all the windows and sing, 'How much is that doggie in the window'.

That afternoon one of the boys had yelled 'Gimme my dog back!' – and the guy couldn't take any more. He rushed out and leaped on to the bus, grabbed the kid by the scruff of the neck and shook him. Jonathan said he wished he'd been there to see it. I bet he would.

Before I went home, I went into the lounge and practised the piano for ten minutes – they always let me. I'd only just started when Mr Miles came in and flopped down in an easy chair, listening, his foot swaying in time to the music. He didn't say much – I wouldn't want him to – but just having him there made me feel that he was really interested in me. For a few minutes I almost wished he was *my* dad.

Jonathan's mum had been rolling out pastry while I'd been admiring their poster. I thought she couldn't possibly have heard what I said because Splodge had been sitting on his dad's knee, bouncing up and down and laughing like crazy. But she must have known I liked it because a few days later she gave me one just like it for my bedroom.

I didn't dare stick pins in the new wallpaper, so I went out and bought some Blu-Tack and stuck it on the back of my bedroom door. It made the room seem more *mine* somehow – and yet, in a way, I didn't want it to be. I wanted Gran to hurry up and get better so that I could go home. And though she was a bit better now (Mother had been good about phoning the hospital every couple of days), I knew I'd be here for a long time. Unless, of course, she'd let me go to Dad's after all. I was missing him.

Every year I usually went to stay with him two or three times. I had my own untidy room in his untidy flat. Why was it suddenly so inconvenient for me to go there? I wondered, suddenly, if Mrs Nosy Fisher really *had* asked if I could stay with him.

'I bet she just *said* that,' I said to the chickens on the poster. 'She knew my mother had decided to have me here, so she didn't even bother mentioning it to my dad. What a mean trick!' I sat down slowly on the bed. What if I went there anyway? For two pins I would. If it wasn't for Jonathan, I told myself. And school . . .

Because school, I had found, wasn't bad at all. I went to Huntley Grange Upper, the same school as Jonathan. But we weren't in the same form. On the very first day I had spotted the grand piano on the stage in the main hall and before long Mrs Richards, the music teacher, said I could practise on it in the lunch-hour.

So I took my music to school and worked my way through all my old favourites: Handel's 'Largo'; Beethoven's 'Moonlight Sonata'; Bach's Two-Part Inventions. Then one day I started on the old stuff my dad liked to play – 'Black and White Rag', and

'Boogamba' and all the rest, and before long I had an audience. Mrs Richards appeared – her pink cheeks pinker than usual – and chivvied them all outside to the playground.

'I think you're going to have to stick to playing something a bit less flamboyant,' she said to me. 'I know I said you could stay in and practise, but we don't want to encourage breaking the school rules, do we?'

I said I was sorry, and that I'd try to stick to quieter music in future. 'It's just so nice to have a good instrument to play – my fingers sort of ran away by themselves.' It seemed a lame excuse, but she just nodded, then sat down and listened for a while.

This time I let my fingers play what they wanted and what I felt. The melody that came was beautiful – but lonely, like a thin, cold wind rippling the faded gorse on the moors. You knew somehow that summer was gone and the year was dying, and winter was almost here.

Mrs Richards said, 'Where did you learn to play like that?'

The bleak wind died to a mere breath of sound; then there was silence.

'I don't remember,' I told her. 'But I've had lessons ever since I was a little girl.' I rubbed my arms. They were cold and goose-pimply, the way they always were when I'd been playing that way.

'You play with your spirit,' she went on. 'Your whole self flows into the music. The real you. What does your music teacher say about your playing?'

'I haven't got one. Not now,' I said bitterly, suddenly remembering Saturday mornings at Miss

Sharman's, and the old lady pushing her slidy spectacles up her nose and saying, 'Let yourself go, girl . . . Set the music free!' Now there was nobody.

'But surely your mother's looking for another teacher for you?' she asked. 'I know you might not be in Thornbridge for very long, but you've got to keep up your studies.'

I shrugged my shoulders as if I didn't really care. 'I've asked her,' I said. 'But she doesn't want me to play. And we haven't got a piano.'

Mrs Richards was silent for a moment. 'Has she ever heard you play?' she asked.

I thought back. I didn't think she ever had − not since I learned to play 'Chopsticks' when I was four years old. She'd never wanted to. I shook my head.

'Well, that's it, then,' said Mrs Richards. 'Perhaps I could call in and have a chat with her.' She pushed back her hair and smiled across at me. 'We'll soon get you going again. And until then, keep practising your scales! They're not as exciting as "Black and White Rag", but you can't be a pianist without them!'

She came the same day. The dishwasher was merrily churning away − we only set it going once a day, after tea, and we did all the lot at one go. I had my homework spread out on the kitchen table. 'Agriculture in the Eighteenth Century' I wrote, underlined it, then sat chewing the end of my pen, waiting for inspiration to come.

It didn't. My brain refused to concentrate on history, and instead I was back in the school hall at lunchtime.

'Your whole self flows into the music,' Mrs

Richards had said. The fact that she allowed me to practise on the grand piano said something else about what she thought of my playing. Gran had sent me to piano lessons when I was little, and when I played she used to say, 'You take after your father.' I'd always taken music for granted, like fresh air and sunshine. But lots of people learn the piano. Was I any better than they were? I tried to imagine myself on a stage, a concert pianist in a long white dress. No – that wasn't me at all. Perhaps I'd compose instead and see my name in lights: 'Sandra Harland's Hit Musical'.

Sandra Harland. I came to earth with a bump. Who ever heard of a composer with such an ordinary name? How could any parents give a kid a name like Sandra? But I could always change it later on. I'd choose something stunningly romantic. Cleo? Too short. Tamara, then, or Jessica. Jessica Harland? Not bad. I wrote it in the margin of my history book to see how it looked: 'Jessica Harland's latest hit musical'.

The door-bell rang, and I heard my mother go to answer it. I sighed, and looked again at the heading I had written. What did I know about eighteenth-century agriculture? Just about enough to fit on a postage stamp. A minute or two later my mother poked her head around the kitchen door.

'Your teacher's here, Sandie,' she said. She looked worried. 'You're not in any trouble at school, are you?'

My heart beat a bit faster. Had she really come? Would she be able to talk my mother round? Slowly I went through into the lounge.

'Hi, Sandie,' said Mrs Richards brightly. 'I was passing by so I thought I'd call in and have a word with your mother.'

'What's she been up to?' my mother said. 'I hope she's . . .'

Mrs Richards held up a well-manicured hand. 'Oh, no, no – nothing like that. No.'

She sat on the edge of her chair and examined her fingernails, obviously wondering how to come to the point.

She started again. 'Mrs Harland, I teach music and drama at Sandie's school, you know.'

My mother's raised eyebrows said no, she didn't know.

'I'd better come right to the point. Sandie was playing for me at lunchtime today.'

'Oh yes?' There was an iciness in those two words, but Mrs Richards went on.

'I understand that you haven't yet arranged for her to have piano lessons in Thornbridge. I've got a lot of contacts, and I wondered if I could be of any help?'

'Thank you, no,' my mother said, coldly polite, but smiling. 'I would rather she spent her time learning something useful. As it is, she wastes far too much time up in her bedroom playing her guitar. This music thing is just a phase she's going through. You know what teenagers are like. By next year it'll be tennis. Or horse-riding.'

Mrs Richards uncrossed her legs and leaned forward on her seat. 'But, Mrs Harland – you don't understand. Sandie's something special. Her technique's good, and her playing shows a rare maturity for someone her age . . . I'm sure that, once you've heard her play, you'll change your mind. She could go far.'

That did it.

'*You* don't understand, Mrs Richards,' my mother said, her voice losing some of its politeness. 'My daughter is *not* going to be a musician.'

'I'd be very willing to teach her myself,' Mrs Richards persisted. 'And if it's a matter of finance – though I can hardly think that – I'd be prepared to give her lessons free of charge. Do, please, think about it.'

'Thank you, but that won't be necessary.'

Then I decided to open my mouth. 'You see, Mrs Richards. There was no point in coming here,' I said bitterly. 'It was a waste of time. *She* won't let me play, now or ever.'

'But *why*?' Mrs Richards flushed angrily. She turned to my mother. 'Surely you want Sandie to do well, and make something of herself, Mrs Harland? I simply can't understand your attitude!'

'She could tell you – but she won't!' I burst out.

'Sandie – that will do. Show your teacher out, dear, will you? Thank you for your interest, Mrs Richards, it was very kind of you to call in.'

That was obviously my mother's last word. Mrs Richards stalked to the door, not waiting for me.

'You're making a terrible mistake, Mrs Harland,' she said as she went out.

That night I lay awake for a long time, thinking about my father. Staring angrily into the darkness. He wouldn't turn down an offer like that. *He* would have been delighted to hear Mrs Richards praise his daughter's piano-playing.

How could I bear to stay here one more day? I thought for a long time. And before I went to sleep I had made up my mind.

CHAPTER SIX

My mother was in a hurry.

'Sandie – put the kettle on, please. I'll have a quick coffee before I leave . . . These fashion shows at "Creation Marie" are always the same. It'll be half past eleven before they think of offering coffee to anyone.'

She flung a spoonful of instant coffee into a cup and added a sweetener, then glanced at the clock.

'Today of all days I had to forget to set my alarm. At least I don't have to clean my shoes, I did them last night. And that reminds me, Sandie – do be more careful what you're doing. There was black polish all over the shoe-brush. What a mess – it took me ages to get the stuff off my hands!'

'Sorry. I dropped the brush and it landed in the tin. I meant to clean it off but I forgot.'

'Really, Sandie – you're the limit. You really couldn't care less, could you? You just sail through life leaving other people to tidy up after you. It's the same with your bedroom – I put your clean school blouse in the drawer last night, and it looks as if you've been stirring a pudding in there! There's not much point in ironing clothes at all if you're going to treat them like that.'

'Well, I ironed them myself.'

'And you'll have to iron them again, won't you?

Honestly – I never knew a girl like you. That lovely bedroom looks like a jumble sale. Clothes just dumped on the chair, papers and books all over the floor. You never even make your bed, and I'm blowed if I'm going to start doing it. It's time you acted your age.'

I sat at the table reading the morning paper and pretending not to listen. I was very good at that. My mother was always going on about how untidy I was. Dad never cared what I did with my bedroom when I was staying with him. He was as bad as I was. A whole week's papers scattered around the room. Dirty dishes piled in the sink. Dust on the mantelpiece. Empty coffee cups all over the place that left sticky rings behind when you picked them up. But we always muddled through somehow. It didn't look so good – but life was a lot more comfortable.

It was eight-fifteen when my mother finally left. I watched her back the car out of the drive with a feeling of satisfaction, my head buzzing with plans of my own. Two minutes later I was up in my bedroom changing out of my school clothes. Then I stood on a chair, dragged my suitcase off the top of the wardrobe and began throwing things in, all higgledy-piggledy.

I had thought it all out in bed last night. I reckoned that if I just turned up at Dad's flat, my mother and her boyfriend wouldn't be able to do anything about it, because Dad would be sure to want me to stay.

'You should have come here in the first place,' he'd say to me, and everything would be all right. He'd ring my mother and tell her where I was, and

44

tell her I would be staying with him. He'd arrange a school for me, and piano lessons – perhaps he'd even find the time to give me lessons himself. I'd like that; the two of us sitting at the piano, working together. We'd play duets, like we used to do when I was small, and he'd tell me I wasn't doing badly.

The door-bell rang. I glanced at my watch. It was half past eight. Blow – I'd forgotten about Jonathan. He usually called for me about now so we could walk down to school together. I hesitated. I thought about ignoring the bell so that he'd think I'd already gone. But I didn't. When it rang again I ran down and flung the door open.

He stood on the doorstep staring at me.

'Why aren't you ready for school?' he asked. 'Are you going out somewhere?'

I could have said I was ill, or that I was going to the dentist's, and he'd have gone away. I don't really know why, but I told him the truth.

'I'm going to my dad's,' I said. 'I'm just packing my case.'

'How did you manage to persuade her to let you go?'

I looked away. 'I didn't ask her.'

He followed me into the kitchen. 'So she doesn't know you're going?' He looked shocked. 'But you can't just go off like that, without telling her. She'll be worried when she comes home and you're not here.'

'Her, worry?' I said. 'Don't make me laugh! And don't look at me like that – she really doesn't care, you know. You should have heard her talking to Mrs Richards last night, telling her that music was just a phase I was going through, and that she'll

45

never allow me to be a musician. Most parents *encourage* their kids to do what they're good at . . . I can't understand her.'

'I don't suppose you really *want* to understand her. It seems a bit tough on you, but she must have a good reason for being like that.'

I sniffed. 'It's because my dad's a musician. I can't think of any other reason. She hates him, and she doesn't want me reminding her of him all the time.'

'Look – why don't you try talking to her? I mean, really talking – without turning it into a row. Try to understand her side of it.'

'I won't be around to do any talking,' I said firmly. 'I'll be at my dad's flat. Look – it's all right for you. You've got a nice family. You've got plenty of friends in your church, and all that. Nobody tries to stop you doing what you're good at. *Your* mother doesn't nag all the time. She's nice. I wish she was *my* mum.'

'Dumbo! Problem-free living! Is that what you really think? That Christians have it easy all the time?'

'OK, OK. There's no need to get mad.'

'Who's mad? It's just that you seem to have this dumb idea that life is plain sailing for everybody but you! You should have been around when my dad lost his job a couple of years ago – his company closed down, right out of the blue! Don't think that was easy!'

'I don't. I never said so. But if life isn't any easier when you're a Christian, I don't see why you want to bother being one.'

Jonathan perched on one of the breakfast bar

stools and messed about with the salt-pot. 'It might not be easier, but it's different, and better. When you belong to Jesus he's there with you – inside you – all the time. He never goes away. You know he's on your side, somehow.'

I said, 'Pie in the sky!' But all the same, I couldn't help wishing he was right.

'Sandie – if you were a Christian, things could be a lot better between you and your mum.'

'And if I had wings, I could fly. Besides, it's a bit late for that,' I said. 'You've forgotten. I won't *be* here, clever-clogs.'

'I don't think you should go.' Jonathan looked stubborn. 'I think you should stay and work things out. Running away won't solve anything.'

'And I think you should mind your own business.' I pointed to the clock on the wall. 'Have you seen the time?' I said. 'You're going to be late for school – you'll have to run.'

Jonathan picked up his bag. 'You've got my phone number,' he said. 'Will you let me know what happens?'

'If you want me to. Look, Jonathan – give my love to your mother, won't you? Tell her . . . tell her I'm taking the poster with me.' I don't know why I wanted her to know that.

He nodded, and was gone.

I stood for a long time, thinking. What if he was right? What if I *was* making a mistake? Perhaps I should stay on a bit longer. Give God – and my mother – a chance.

But what chance had my mother given me? None at all, unless I fitted into the mould she had made for me. Nice clothes, tidy hair, and when I left school, a career in the fashion business. But what about my music? I simply *had* to play. She didn't understand, and I couldn't explain, that music was like a fire burning inside me. I had no choice – I had to let it come out.

I went slowly back upstairs. I finished my packing and shut up my guitar in its case again. I got together all the money I had – Dad sent me some every month, so I was never short of cash like some of the kids I knew. After that I rang the bus station. I found I'd just missed a Leeds bus, but there was another at eleven o'clock. I meant to be on it.

The bus took ages. First of all it was late setting off, and then we toured around every village in Yorkshire – or so it seemed – picking up passengers. It was long after dinner-time when we reached Leeds, and I was ravenous – I'd forgotten to take something to eat. My stomach kept making disgusting gurgling noises, and I hoped nobody else would notice. Even when we got there the journey wasn't over; there was still another bus to catch – Dad's flat was three or four miles out of the city.

I got off at the bottom of Arbour Road. I was glad Dad lived in a nice district. His flat was at the top of a long road of fancy houses with big gardens. It was a drag, carrying the suitcase and the guitar – they weren't so much heavy as awkward to carry – and my arms were aching by the time I reached the first of the square, modern blocks of flats. But as I got nearer my feet carried me faster and faster, and I felt happier than I'd felt all day. There was Boswell House. Then Walpole and Johnson – and then Congreve House. That was the one. The lift was too slow for me, and I ran eagerly through the hallway, down the passage and up the stairs.

Dad was out.

I'd never thought of that. I sat on my case outside his locked door and buried my head in my arms. I could have cried – and my eyes did leak a few drops before I remembered Mrs Greenwood. She was the old lady who lived across the landing – the one who used to sit with me when Dad was out at work. I knew she had his spare key for emergencies. I reckoned this was an emergency.

I ran across and knocked on her door.

After a minute she answered me. Her voice was frail and shaky. 'Who is it?'

'It's me. Sandie Harland. You remember me, Mrs Greenwood?'

'Just a minute.'

I waited impatiently while the old lady fiddled with locks and bolts and chains – her place was like Fort Knox. She got the door open at last.

'Come in, dearie, come in. It's nice to see you. You must excuse the mess.' She picked up a plate and a mug and took them away to the kitchen. She used a stick now, I noticed. She never used to.

'My, how you've grown,' she went on, lowering herself carefully into a chair. 'I wouldn't have known you, you've changed so much. You're quite a young lady now.'

There was a mirror in the room, and I couldn't help glancing at myself. She was right. I did look different. Older – and better. It's amazing what a nice dress can do for you.

'Would you like a cup of tea?' she asked. 'It won't take a minute . . . I'll just go and put the kettle on.'

'Oh – no, thanks,' I said hastily. 'I just called in to borrow Dad's door key. I'm locked out and I don't know how long he'll be.'

'I saw him this morning, and he never said you were coming,' she said.

I said nothing to that.

'He always used to let me know. "How do you fancy baby-sitting next week?" he'd say. And I'd know he was expecting you.' The old lady chuckled. 'We've had some good games of Happy Families, you and me, haven't we? Waiting for your dad to come home from work. You'll be too old for that now. Too old until you're as old as I am!'

She opened the big old-fashioned cupboard in the corner of the room, took down a china teapot with blue dragons on it and fished out a small bunch of keys.

'There you are, dearie,' she said, handing them over. 'This big one's the key to his flat. I don't know where he can be – it's not like him to be out when he knows you're coming.'

I thanked her, and hurried away. My stomach was growling and I couldn't wait to get at Dad's fridge. He never kept much food in the house – he ate out a lot – but at least I'd be able to fix myself a cheese sandwich.

I let myself in, shut the door with my behind and dumped my gear on the floor. I walked through the hall and opened the living-room door – and then stared around in bewilderment.

Everything was different. I had to be in the wrong flat. How could I have made a mistake like that? I turned back to the door, then stopped again.

If this wasn't Dad's flat, then how come the key fitted the door?

CHAPTER SEVEN

I looked around again. That wasn't Dad's three-piece suite. His was an old orange stripey one, with worn patches on all the arms. This one was new; brown, with a flower pattern. And there was a glass-topped coffee table in front of it that I knew I'd never seen before. But the table and chairs under the window were the same — and the picture of horses in the sea was still there, over the mantelpiece.

I relaxed. That was it — he'd simply bought himself some new furniture. Not before time. And yet there was something else, too. I couldn't put my finger on it, but the place was different. It even *smelled* different — what *was* that smell? I sniffed the air. Lavender polish. That was it!

I looked around again doubtfully. Since when had my dad used polish? He hardly ever used a duster, never mind polish. But there was no dust anywhere. No crumbs on the carpet. No newspapers, music, bills, paperback thrillers or dirty coffee mugs lying around.

I grinned. He'd really been turning over a new leaf! I went through into the kitchen. The washing up had been done, and the worktop wiped clean. There was nothing on it except an empty milk bottle and a catalogue for make-up and perfumes. What would he want with that? There was some cooked ham in the fridge, and a bottle of Coke. I poured myself a glass, buttered some bread, and made a thick sandwich of ham and Branston Pickle. Then I ate bread with honey and peanut butter, and finished off with an apple.

After that I felt better. I wandered back into the living-room, wondering when my dad would be back. Maybe I should have telephoned first, but I'd wanted to surprise him. I hadn't bargained on him being out. I dug out some music and played the piano for an hour, then curled up in one of the new chairs.

I'd just got comfortable when I heard voices on the landing outside. It was my dad, and he had somebody with him. I heard a key turn in the lock, and then a girl's voice said, 'Where in the world did that suitcase come from?'

I got up and went to the living-room door. 'Hi, Dad,' I said. 'Mrs Greenwood lent me a key.' He was as good-looking as ever. Tall and dark and lean. Young for his age.

I had wanted to surprise him, and I'd done it. He was thunderstruck.

'Sandie! What the Hamilton are you doing here? I thought you were with your mother.'

The girl said, 'Jack, who is this?'

Dad ran his fingers through his bushy hair. 'It's my daughter, Sandie,' he told her. 'Sandie, this is a friend, Caroline Webster.'

A friend. That's what my mother had said about Bill. The girl and I eyed each other warily. She was a lot younger than he was: mid-twenties I'd say, and very pretty, with long fair hair like on a shampoo commercial, and big blue eyes. It was easy to see what he saw in her!

She turned abruptly and marched into the kitchen. My dad looked at me and sighed, then went after her and closed the door behind him.

I could still hear their voices, though.

'Your *daughter*, for heaven's sake! You never told me you had a daughter.'

'Caroline, you knew I was divorced from my wife.'

'Sure. You told me all about it – conveniently leaving *her* out of the story! What's she doing here? What are we supposed to do with her? She's obviously come to stay, she's brought her suitcase and everything.'

My cheeks began to burn. Who did she think she was, talking as if she owned the place? Spoiling things between me and Dad . . .

She went on. 'Did you tell her she could come?'

'Of course not. When my mother was taken ill, the neighbour rang and asked if Sandie could come for a while. I said it wasn't a good time just now, and as far as I knew she'd settled in with my ex-wife. Believe me, Caroline – I don't know what she's doing here . . . perhaps they had a row, or something. We'll sort it out, you'll see.'

'Well, you can sort it out without me. Take your pick, Jack, it's me or her. Surely you don't expect me to stay here with your *daughter*, for goodness' sake. One big happy family! Is that what you want?'

'Caroline . . .'

'I'm going out, Jack, and when I come back she'd better be gone. Just get rid of her!'

She was living here. I should have known. As soon as I smelled that polish, I should have known there was a woman here. I didn't want to believe it, but I knew it was true. My dad . . . and *her*. I felt sick suddenly, and sweat came out on my forehead and top lip, and as the kitchen door opened and they came out together, I dashed past them into the bathroom.

I only just made it.

I flushed the loo and sat miserably on the edge of the bath while wave after wave of nausea surged over me. I was sick again. I filled a glass with cold water and sipped at it until I felt a bit better.

Someone tried the door. 'Sandie. Sandie – are you OK?'

No thanks to him. I wiped my mouth with a tissue. 'I'm fine, Dad,' I said.

Still trembling, I went back into the living-room and sat down again. The girl had gone.

'Can I get you anything? A cup of tea?'

I shook my head, dumb with misery.

'You know, you should have phoned to let me know you were coming,' he said awkwardly.

'This Caroline – are you going to marry her?'

'Good grief, no. Once was enough – you ask your mother. I'm not the marrying kind.'

'My mother's got a boyfriend.' I don't know why I told him that.

'Good for her.'

'He's called Bill. They're getting married in November.' My voice rose. 'At least *they're* not living together. Like you and *her*.'

'That was uncalled for, Sandie. You'll understand when you're older. This is all a part of life.'

I didn't want to understand. I didn't want it to be a part of *my* life. There had to be something better than this kind of thing. It was horrible. My mother and Bill. My dad and this Caroline . . . why did it have to be like this? It should be Mother and Dad, and me.

'Does your mother know where you are?'

I shook my head again.

'I'd better give her a ring. What time does she get back from the shop?'

'Five-ish. Sometimes earlier.'

He dialled the number, and I heard the far-off buzz that was her phone ringing.

'Hello – Louise? Jack here . . . yes, she's here. Thought I'd better let you know.'

I heard my mother's voice at the other end of the line, and my dad fitted words in around what she said.

'Yes . . . yes. Did he? . . . Well, if you think that's the best thing . . . fine. OK, I'll tell her. See you later.'

He put the phone down. 'She already knew you were here – it seems a friend of yours told her when she came home from work.'

Jonathan of course. Bigmouth Miles.

'She's on her way here already. She was just leaving when I rang.'

'You mean, she's coming here? Driving all that way?'

'It's only just over an hour in the car. She knows *I* can't take you back – I start work at seven-thirty.' He looked at his watch. 'We'd better get something to eat, hadn't we?'

'I'm not hungry.'

'You will be. How about a pizza? And some oven chips? There's plenty of stuff in the freezer.'

He got busy in the kitchen. I didn't offer to help. I sat on a chair and stared dismally out of the window. My mother was coming for me. Dad didn't want me to stay, after all. I was just a silly kid who'd done something stupid and upset all his plans. I didn't belong here, any more than I belonged in my mother's neat semi-detached. I'd built up a childish fantasy about my marvellous father, and the wonderful life we'd have together. And my daydreams had been

55

smashed to pieces in less than half an hour. He'd turned out to be as human as anyone else.

Dad tucked into his pizza while I pushed food around my plate.

'How's the music coming on?' he asked.

'It's not. Mother won't let me have lessons – that's what this is all about. Our music teacher at school said she'd teach me herself – but my mother won't hear of it. She says she's no intention of letting me be a musician.'

Dad poured himself a glass of wine. 'Can't say I'm surprised.'

Was that all he had to say? How could he be so cool about it?

'But that's why I came here. I thought I'd be able to stay! I thought I could go to school here, and you'd arrange music lessons for me,' I said. 'I didn't know about Caroline. What will happen now?'

'With Caroline, you mean?'

'Yes.'

'She'll be back . . . Look, I'm sorry you can't stay here. It's a pity you and Louise don't hit it off better, but your gran won't be ill for ever, you know. She's getting well now. All this might not be for much longer. You'll be able to go back home soon.'

He wiped his mouth and pushed his plate away. 'Is that the best you can do with that good pizza? . . . Come on, then. Let's hear you play.' He nodded towards the piano. 'I see you've been having a go at the "Moonlight". Let's hear what you can do.'

He stopped me half-way through the first movement. 'No – don't let that D sharp go. Hold it on – emphasize that . . . D sharp, C sharp, B sharp . . . dum, dum, *dum*,' he sang.

This was just as it should be. Dad and me, together at the piano, just as I'd imagined . . . Only in another hour the dream would be over and I'd be on my way back to Thornbridge. A tear ran down my cheek and plopped right on to middle C. Another one followed it, and I stopped playing to wipe my eyes.

'Hey, Sandie – don't do that. Don't let it get to you.' My dad could never bear to see me cry. 'Look – I've got something that'll cheer you up. I meant to send it through the post, but I might as well give it to you now.'

He held out a square of pink card.

'What is it?' I blew my nose loudly.

'It's a ticket. Have a look.'

It said, in big fancy letters: 'FORCE 7 IN CONCERT', and underneath, in smaller print, 'Also featuring Quicksilver, Jess Dury, Cacique. 5th July, Festival Hall, Parr'.

'We're providing some of the back-up,' he said modestly. 'Free tickets all round. Are you coming?'

I read the ticket through again. 'Of course I'll come. Force 7! I've got all their albums – they're great. And Cacique are good. I don't know about the others. And you'll be on *stage* with them?'

'With some of them,' he said. 'Fame at last.'

The concert was next Thursday. Parr was only a half-hour bus ride from Thornbridge. And Dad would be there. I wasn't exactly on Cloud Nine, but he'd hit on the only thing that could possibly make me feel a bit better.

CHAPTER EIGHT

The more I thought about my mother coming to fetch me, the better I liked the idea. After all, she and Dad had been in love once . . . Now they were going to meet up after all this time, they might fall for each other all over again! It was perfectly possible. I got quite excited about the whole idea.

I was in for another disappointment.

He said she looked marvellous – she was wearing a grey skirt and a long-sleeved pink blouse, with a gorgeous pearly waistcoat. She said he was looking very well, and had he been abroad to get such a fantastic suntan? But they didn't seem especially glad to see each other. They chatted for a few minutes about the weather, and holidays, and how hot Greece had been this year. But all the time they were talking my mother was edging towards the door. I did try, though – to keep them together for a bit longer I offered to make some coffee, but my mother said we had to go.

Dad came out to the car with us, carrying my case. I'd never even opened it. He gave me a big bear-hug and pressed a five-pound note into my hand, then kissed my mother – on her forehead, for goodness' sake! I couldn't help wondering if things might have been different if there hadn't been Bill. Or Caroline.

If only Mother and Dad had never split up. We

could have been a proper family, and done things together. It could have been so different . . . I might even have had brothers and sisters! A little Splodge of my own. And I would have really *belonged*. Gran and Gramps were my family, but even there I sometimes had this feeling of not really belonging. Six months with them, then off to Dad's for a few weeks, then back to Gran's again at the end of the holidays. And an occasional stint with my mother in between. It had been like that ever since I was little – and now it was worse. I still didn't belong anywhere, but now I was old enough to see why. You've heard of square pegs in round holes? Well, that was me.

I thought of Jonathan and his family. They did things together – swimming, and flying kites, and having barbecues in the back garden. And they were always laughing at something, even if it was only the silly adverts on the telly. Families ought to be like that.

Of course, according to Jonathan, it was the religious bit that made the difference. Being a Christian. Belonging to Jesus—that's how he'd described it.

I remembered the poster: 'He will cover me with his wings; I will be safe in his care'. Knowing Jesus for yourself would be like that. You'd feel safe, and loved, and secure. Kind of *under cover*. Suddenly, I wished it could be like that for me.

'Well, Sandie, I hope you're quite satisfied.' My mother's voice broke into my thoughts, and I realized that neither of us had said a word since we set off.

'I was worried sick about you, do you know that? What in the world made you do such a thing? To go off like that, without even leaving a note . . . If Jonathan hadn't come over to tell me what had happened, I'd have been down at the police station. I didn't know what to think!'

I didn't feel like having another row. 'I'm sorry. But Dad would have rung you. He *did* ring you.'

'For his own convenience, yes,' she said drily. 'He's very good at putting himself first.'

I almost gave her a sharp answer, and then didn't. Because I was finding out that it was quite true. Today I'd seen something in my father that I'd never seen before. I wondered what the real reason was why they'd split up. We sat in silence for a while. Did I dare ask her about it? After all, I was their daughter. I *ought* to know the truth. I took a deep breath and said, 'Why did you and Dad get divorced?'

She gave me the standard reply. 'We were better off apart.'

'No. I mean *why*. What happened between you two? Couldn't you stand his job? Couldn't he stand your cooking? What was it? I've got a right to know!'

'I've always thought you had a right *not* to know. Sandie. I've tried to protect you from the truth. I've never called your father names in front of you – in fact I've hardly spoken of him at all. You've been happier not knowing about it.'

I doubted it. 'Even if it was something horrible, I still want to know.'

It was more horrible than I'd imagined.

'There was a girl,' she said after a minute. She drove fast, overtaking a furniture van, then pulling in to the left again. 'This girl sang with your father's band, and played the guitar, too. Frances, her name was. You were just a toddler, and I was tied up with looking after you. But Frances had plenty of time to give your father. She was prettier, too, than I was.'

I sat very still, gripping the seat-belt as hard as I could to keep my hands from trembling. I wanted to cry out, to stop her saying those things about my father. I wanted this to be all lies—something she'd made up to get back at him. But I only had to look at her face to know that it was all true.

'So you divorced him.'

'Not straight away. Not until after he'd gone off and left me.'

It was true, then, what Bill had said.

'But surely, there was something you could have done? You could have tried a bit harder. Worked something out together?'

'Maybe. If it had been just once. But after Frances there was Betty . . . or was it Anne? I can't remember.' Her voice was cool. Bitter. 'It was his job, you see. He was the fascinating celebrity – the star of the show! There was always some pretty girl ready to fall for his handsome face.'

There still was. I wondered if she knew about Caroline.

'But he had you. You're not bad looking, Mother – and you were younger then!'

'Thanks for the compliment. But I wasn't glamorous enough in those days. I was there to keep the place clean and tidy, and cook his meals, and look after his child. Oh – I'm not blaming you, Sandie – how could it possibly be your fault? But after the divorce, I was determined to get my self-respect back. To make something of myself – he'd made me feel so small, you see. It's not much fun being rejected by a man like your father. Somehow, you got left out of things . . . Jack's parents were willing to keep you with them. It seemed the best thing to do at the time. It's not much use now wishing that things had been different.'

'Do you hate him?'

'I tried to, for a long time, but I really loved him, you see. It's not so easy to turn love into hate.'

'But what about now? I mean, you and Bill . . .'

'Now I love Bill. It's as simple as that. And Bill's a man who's worth being in love with. He's worth ten of your father. I wish you'd give him a chance, Sandie.'

I thought of Bill, with his pink shiny scalp showing through his wispy hair. And his baggy trousers, and his stomach just starting to bulge over his belt. How could she be in love with a man who looked like that? Nobody could be less like my dad. But perhaps that was the reason?

I had time to do some thinking as we drove home. Perhaps my mother was right about me and Bill. I really hadn't given him a chance. I'd taken a dislike to him the first time I'd seen him, and I'd let him know it, too. We'd started off all wrong, and I didn't know if we could ever get over that. But now I decided that I'd try to be polite to him. Anyway, Bill might be an ally worth having – after all, he wouldn't be so much against me playing the piano. Maybe he'd even be able to talk my mother round!

Knowing the truth about my dad helped me to understand why she was set against me being a musician. As far as she was concerned, the whole music scene had ruined her life – and here was her daughter wanting to go into it too! No wonder she was bitter.

But I can't help being what I am, I thought. *Even knowing all that can't change me*. There had to be a way to show her that I could be a musician and still be normal.

Bill was in the house, waiting for us, when we got back.

'Hello, Bill,' I said.

He stared at me. Then he took his glasses off and stared some more. 'Well,' he said, 'that beats all! You've had your mother out of her mind with worry — finding you and all your clothes missing and your suitcase gone. She was on the verge of going to the police to report you missing when some kid told her where you were. So she drives all the way to Yorkshire to pick you up, and then all the way back again — and you breeze in here as cool as a cucumber and say "Hello, Bill"!'

My lower lip trembled, but I refused to cry in front of him. I glared back at him, hating his piggy eyes and his pink scalp and his long nose. How could I have thought of making a friend of him?

'Just what have you to say for yourself, young lady?'

I pursed my lips together and walked past him into the kitchen. I filled up the kettle and put coffee into two cups. If he wanted one, he could make his own.

He caught hold of my shoulder and spun me around. 'I want you to apologize to your mother!'

She was standing in the doorway. 'Bill — don't!'

'Don't touch me, you fat pig!' I shouted. 'You don't have any right to talk to me like that. You don't own me, and you don't own my mother either. I don't have to do a single thing you tell me.'

He let go of me as if I was something that had crawled out from under a stone. He turned to my mother. 'Louise, you're crazy to want her here. She's nothing but a spoiled, undisciplined, selfish brat. As soon as her grandmother is well enough, I want you to promise to send her back. We can't have her here with us.'

'Who wants to live with *you*?' I shouted, trembling with fury. 'You make me sick! I just can't wait to get away from here!'

I ran out of the back door, down the garden, over the fence, and straight through the Miles' door without knocking. And then I burst into tears.

CHAPTER NINE

'Hi, Sandie,' Mr Miles said cheerfully – then he saw my face and added, 'Hey – what's up?' But I just shook my head. I couldn't say anything. Jonathan's mum was washing dishes, but she dried her hands and took me through into the lounge. We sat on the couch and she put her arms around me, and I cried as if I was five years old again.

I fished in my pocket for a hanky and couldn't find one. I sniffed, and wiped my eyes with the back of my hand. Mrs Miles went out of the room and came back with a box of tissues.

'Feeling better?' she asked as I blew my nose.

I shook my head. Nothing would ever make me feel better.

'Do you want to talk about it?'

I didn't, really. But once I'd started, I found I couldn't stop. I told her, first of all, about my dad and Caroline.

'Finding out like that – it was horrible. I threw up in the bathroom,' I told her, and felt my stomach turn over again at the memory. I could hear the girl's horrified voice now: 'What's *she* doing here? . . . Take your pick, Jack – it's her or me . . . Get rid of her.'

And he'd picked Caroline. That's what had hurt so much. He'd rather have her than me. Had my mother felt like that about Frances? Frances and Betty and the others.

I could tell that Mrs Miles knew how I felt, although she didn't say anything. She just stroked my hair and let me talk, in bits and pieces, as things came into my mind.

I told her about Bill. 'I can't stand him, but my mother asked me to be nice to him. She said he was worth ten of my dad, and I hadn't given him a chance. And I was going to try − honestly. But as soon as we walked through the door he was down on me like a ton of bricks because I'd gone off to Dad's this morning.'

'And what happened?'

'I lost my temper. I called him a fat pig . . . I don't know what made me say that. I've made things worse than they were before − and I can't seem to help myself! I never used to be like this!' I dabbed at my eyes again with the soggy tissue.

She squeezed my shoulder. 'Well, we all say things we don't mean, Sandie. Especially when we're upset. It must have been horrible for you, finding out like that about your mum and dad, on top of worrying about your grandma, and everything. Is she getting better?'

'Yes. Gramps rings every time he goes to see her. She's getting the use of her leg back again, and she's having physiotherapy − exercises and all that, to help her to learn to walk again, and use her arm too.'

'Are you looking forward to going back home?'

Of course I was. It would be lovely to see Gran and Gramps again. And yet . . . Another tear slid across my face and dripped from the end of my nose.

'What is it?'

I shook my head. 'I don't know.' But then I put the feeling into words. 'It was when you talked about going home. It's just that . . . I don't feel as though I belong anywhere.'

I remembered something that happened when I was small. I'd wandered off by myself, and somehow got inside a school. It must have been Croxley comprehensive, but I didn't know that then, of course. Everyone had gone home, and it was empty and echoing, and full of shadows, and I couldn't lift the heavy bar to open the door. I was frightened of the emptiness and I sat in a corner on the floor and cried until the caretaker found me and took me home.

And now I felt like that again. Lost and lonely and frightened.

I said, 'I can't wait to be grown up.'

Mrs Miles smiled. 'Most youngsters can't.'

'But some day I'll get married and have some children of my own – and then I'll belong to a proper family.'

'You don't have to wait until you're grown up to belong to a family, you know,' she said. 'You don't even have to wait until tomorrow. You could be in God's family straight away – today. And that's not just a romantic idea dreamed up by some preacher for his Sunday sermon. It's true.'

'But how?' Having tomorrow today still sounded like story-book stuff, and I still couldn't see how being a Christian could make any real difference to a person's life. Your problems would still be there. You'd still have divorced parents. You'd still have to live with people you didn't get on with, who wouldn't let you do what you wanted to do.

'When you're born as a baby you have a mum and a dad and, if you're lucky, a family. But God offers us the chance to be "born again" when we believe in Jesus. You become God's child, with a whole new life and a whole new family – that's what the church is all about.'

'So you can't be a Christian without going to church,' I said, screwing up my nose. I couldn't help it. It sounded about as exciting as yesterday's rice pudding.

'That's not what I said! The church isn't a place you *go* to – it's a big family that you *belong* to! All real Christians, everywhere, are part of the church. It's like a body, with arms and legs, and teeth and toenails – we're all a small part of the same body.'

'But *you* go to church every Sunday,' I reminded her.

'Well, when you get to know God you want to spend time with him and with the rest of his family – and so do a lot of other people. So we get together to do it, that's all! And by going to a church meeting, the Christians in God's family can really get to know each other. In our church, everyone helps everyone else. We go shopping for the old people and we babysit for the younger ones. We help each other with jobs like decorating or digging gardens. It's because we really *care* about each other. It's just like a family ought to be. If I was ill tomorrow, I can think straight away of half a dozen people who'd look after Splodge for me. Being in a family like that, with God as the Father, makes you feel safe and secure.'

It sounded good. 'Like the poster,' I said.

She knew straight away what I meant. 'That's it exactly. Just like the chicks sheltering under the mother hen's wings.'

' "He will cover me with his wings; I will be safe in his care",' I whispered. I had that bit off by heart by now. 'Is that in the Bible?'

'Yes. It comes in one of the psalms. Have you got a Bible at home?'

I shook my head. I couldn't ever remember seeing one at my mother's house. She didn't have many books of any kind. Just fashion magazines.

'I'll give you Jonathan's old one – I know he won't mind. He had a new one at Christmas.'

She went out, and came back a minute or two later with a book in her hand. 'It's a bit dog-eared, but it'll do to begin with,' she said. 'I'll make a note of the verse about the chickens and then you can read it for yourself. Now – Jonathan's got the computer set up out there. What about a game before you go home? Go and put him out of his misery, will you?'

I didn't really feel like it. And besides, I had a bone to pick with him. But I went anyway.

He grinned at me as I went through the door, and I sniffed and said, 'Supergrass!'

He knew what I meant, but he kept on grinning. 'Don't be daft,' he said. 'I *had* to tell her. You know why.'

'Hmph.' I knew he was right, but I hadn't intended letting him off so easily.

He rolled his eyes round and round, and I grinned in spite of myself. You couldn't stay mad at Jonathan for very long. 'Come and play "Double Agent",' he said. 'We'll take it in turns, and see who wins the most games.'

I hesitated.

'Come on.'

'Oh, all right, then,' I said.

But I simply couldn't concentrate. My spies were all shot and Jonathan won every game.

When I got back home, Bill was still there. He and my mother were sitting very close together on the couch watching a film on the telly. He didn't turn around when I went in, but I knew he was still mad at me – the tips of his ears had turned dark pink. I knew I couldn't truly call myself a Christian yet, but I said to him, 'I'm sorry for what I called you, Bill.' And then I went up to bed.

I didn't think I could possibly go to sleep, but I did. I dropped off straight away – and then woke up much later, feeling cold. The wind had got up – the window was open and rattling about on its catch, and the curtains were billowing out like pale, wriggling ghosts. Spears of rain stabbed against the glass with a noise like someone throwing handfuls of gravel. I slid out of bed and shut the window. A lot of rain had come in and the carpet was damp. Who'd have thought it was July?

I huddled into a tight ball under my quilt, screwed up my cold toes and shut my eyes. But this time I didn't sleep.

Today . . . no, yesterday – it was twenty past three in the morning – had been an awful day. I kept on seeing that girl.

'It's her or me, Jack . . .' The words went round and round in my head. And my dad. Apologetic, but never for a minute thinking of throwing *her* out so that his daughter could stay. Tears prickled behind my eyelids. He was a traitor. And yet he was my dad, who'd sat me on his knee at the piano and taught me to play 'The Fairy's Garden', and read me 'Milly Molly Mandy' stories, and taught me to ride a bike.

Someone had once called him 'a lovable rogue'. I'd laughed then, but now I knew it was a good description. He was a traitor, but I loved him anyway.

I couldn't hold back the tears any more, and trying to swallow the lump in my throat, I turned over and cried into my pillow. I cried for my dad and the way he'd betrayed my mother and me; I cried for my gran, and for the way Gramps had looked, the day she went to hospital. I cried for myself and my music and most of all, for my shattered dreams. A childish fantasy I'd had of what might have been.

In the end I slept, with the quilt pulled up around my ears, and my face buried in the wet pillow.

My mother shook me awake the next morning. I surfaced with a blinding headache and swollen eyes, knowing that I had overslept. I'd have to hurry or I'd be late for school. I sat up slowly, feeling as if I'd been through a mincing machine, and crawled out of bed.

'Come on, Sandie – you'll have to move faster than that. Just look at the time! Didn't your alarm go off?'

She picked it up and shook it, and it whirred into life, drilling into my skull like a steam-hammer. She flicked it off again.

'It *must* have gone off,' she said, 'it had nearly run down. How you can sleep through that racket I'll never know. What's this?'

She picked up my concert ticket. I'd left it propped against the bedside lamp. I leaned over and grabbed it from her.

'Dad gave it to me. Force 7 are playing in Parr on Thursday night. You know – the ones on the *Stand by me* album. Dad's providing some of the back-up, and all the musicians got tickets for their families.'

'I hope you're not seriously thinking of going?'

Of course I was. Very seriously. I said, 'Why shouldn't I go?'

'After all that happened yesterday, you can ask me that? I thought you'd have seen enough of him to last you at least a year.'

'It's not just because of Dad. I like the group, they're good. And they're playing in *Parr*. It's only a few miles away. How often do you get to see a top group like Force 7? I won't get another chance like this!'

'You won't get this one either. I don't want you going to rock concerts — especially on your own. It won't finish till goodness knows what time — and you'd have to be up for school the morning after. Even if you went, he'd be too busy to talk to you. And, anyway, he'll have his latest flame there, making eyes at him all night.'

So she did know about Caroline. Well, so what? I said, 'That's the real reason you don't want me to go, isn't it? Well, it doesn't make any difference to me. I don't care whether she's there or not — I still want to go.'

'What you want has nothing to do with it, Sandie. You can forget about this concert, because you are not going. And that's final!'

She whisked out of the room, shutting the door harder than necessary.

I stared after her, feeling my cheeks grow bright red, and clenching my hands so tightly I made rows of deep nail-prints in my palms.

Adults can do anything. Any rotten thing they like.

I looked again at my precious concert ticket. She knew I really wanted to go. Why did she always have to spoil things for me?

Well, this time she wouldn't succeed, because I was going anyway.

CHAPTER TEN

I didn't tell anybody what I was planning, not even Jonathan. I knew I'd be in trouble afterwards, but my mother could say what she liked then. By that time it wouldn't matter, because I'd have already been to the concert. Nothing mattered except getting there. I secretly found out the times of the buses and made some other devious plans.

I wangled an invitation to go to Jonathan's for tea. If my mother thought I was over there for the evening it would be quite late before she even thought of worrying about me. And this time I'd leave a note on my dressing-table, telling her where I was − I knew she wouldn't go into my room until she actually started looking for me.

It all went like clockwork. I put on my new pink dress and my black beads, and the black shoes with little heels that my mother had bought me. The effect was amazing. I wasn't a scruffy little kid any more. I looked my age. Perhaps people would think I was even older. I hoped they would.

I thought my mother might have guessed, seeing me dressed up like that just to go to Jonathan's. But she didn't suspect a thing. She just said how nice I looked, and she was glad I was beginning to care about what I looked like. I felt a bit of a louse, but whatever it took, I meant to get to that concert.

I left Jonathan's soon after tea. Mrs Miles was a bit surprised, but I told her I had some homework to do, and she didn't say anything. I went out of their back door as if I was going home, then, my heart hammering, doubled back and sneaked round the side of the house. I hurried past the front window, along the terrace and turned right down Pagett Road. The bus for Parr was already standing in the bus station. I went upstairs and right down to the front, hoping nobody I knew had seen me. I didn't feel safe until the driver started up his engine and moved out into the main road. I sat back with a sigh of relief, and was surprised to find that I was trembling and the palms of my hands were all sweaty.

The Festival Hall was packed. But I had a good seat, four rows from the front. I looked for my dad, but I couldn't see him. I saw Caroline, though. She was sitting right in the middle of the front row with another girl. She was dressed all wrong for this kind of thing, in a posh navy blue dress with a big white collar.

Quicksilver played first. They weren't very good. The lead vocalist sang off-key and sprang around the stage like a frog on a lily-pond. They didn't get much applause.

After that, Jess Dury came on. He was a good singer, but I hardly heard him, because I'd seen my dad. He was at the side of the stage, playing a synthesizer. He was good, too – I'd only ever heard him play the piano. I just wished I could have a go on the synth. I knew that at the end of the first number he'd look around for me, and my heart beat a bit faster. Then he'd know I was there, that I'd used the ticket he'd given me.

Jess Dury bowed, and I clapped until my hands tingled – not for him but for his synth. player. Dad turned and scanned the audience. His eyes found Caroline and they exchanged a long look. She nudged the girl next to her and they whispered to each other. My stomach turned over as if I'd eaten a pound of chocolate creams, and I stopped clapping suddenly. Then he was looking for me. He gave me a wide, twinkling smile, and nodded his head, but my face felt as if it was made of wood. I couldn't have smiled for a million pounds.

Half-way through Cacique's performance I pulled myself together. I'd risked a lot to come to this concert. I'd schemed and plotted and told lies so that I could enjoy a good night out. I decided to enjoy it or die trying.

At last it was Force 7's turn. There was a lot of clapping and stamping. I clapped and stamped and jumped up and down along with everyone else, and screamed until my throat was sore. They were marvellous.

Caroline didn't seem to think so though. She was sitting back in her seat and looking thoroughly bored. I saw her look at her watch. I didn't know why she'd bothered coming – she wasn't interested in my dad because of his music, I could see that!

The group played on and on, and got louder and louder. We clapped them again and again. They left the stage, and came back to do another number, and then another. When they went off for the last time, there was a rush for the exits. It took a long time for everybody to get out of the hall, and I was one of the last, hanging on just in case my dad came looking for me. He didn't, and there was no sign of Caroline and her friend.

Outside it was dark, and chilly too. I was glad I'd brought my jacket, though the bus stop was only down the road. I ran to keep warm and my feet beat time to the rhythm of the music still thumping in my head.

The town hall came into view as I turned the corner, and one look at the clock brought me to an abrupt standstill. I stared at it, appalled. It was ten past twelve.

No point now in running for a bus – the last one left an hour ago! What was I going to do? I went back the way I'd come. There were still groups of kids in front of the hall, laughing and making a lot of noise.

I went up the steps but a man in a brown uniform stopped me at the door.

'You left something behind?' He sounded suspicious.

'No – I wanted to see if my dad was still here . . .'

'Nobody's here.'

'But he was playing in the band.'

He smiled, not believing me. I think he thought I was an autograph hunter. 'I told you. Nobody's here. The musicians have all left as well, so hop it.'

I turned and went slowly back down the steps. Half an hour on the bus. How many miles would that be? Nine or ten perhaps. How long would it take me to walk that far? And wearing these silly shoes, too. They were pinching my toes already.

How could I have forgotten the time like that? I hadn't looked at my watch all evening. What would my mother think when I didn't turn up on the last bus? The trouble I'd been in before was nothing to the trouble I was in now.

I wasn't looking where I was going, and I walked

straight into a boy of about eighteen who was clowning about on the pavement with his mates.

'Watch where you're going, can't you?'

I could have said the same thing to him, but I didn't. I walked on. I must have looked miserable because he shouted after me, 'What's up, Doc?' in a Bugs Bunny voice.

I turned around to face him. It wasn't anything to do with him, but I told him anyway. 'I missed my last bus.'

A girl with spiky hair and dangling earrings shaped like parrots mimicked me in a high squeaky voice. 'I missed my last bus!'

'How you going to get home?'

'She's going to fly,' somebody else said.

'Is it a bird? Is it a plane?'

'No – it's the busless hitch-hiker!' finished a tall spotty boy. They all laughed like crazy.

I turned and walked away. The girl shouted, 'Where do you live?'

I hesitated, then said, 'Thornbridge.'

'You'd better take pity on her, Kev.'

'It's on our way. Come on, we'll run you home.' The boy tossed up an empty beer can and kicked it into the middle of the road.

He looked as though he'd had a few of them, and I didn't particularly want a lift home with this crowd. There didn't seem to be anything else to do, though. I said, 'Will there be room?'

'Stacks,' he said airily. 'You can sit on Nick's knee.'

'You'll love that, Nick.'

'So will she!'

'She doesn't look as though she trusts you, Nick!'

They headed for the car park, shouting and making catcalls, and I trailed miserably along with them.

The car was a posh new Jaguar. I wondered if Kev had borrowed it from his dad — or had he pinched it from somewhere? He revved up the engine while the rest of us piled inside.

I found myself sitting gingerly on the spotty boy's knee — there were four of us squashed into the back, and three more in the front.

We set off with a jerk that threw me back into Nick's arms, then we lurched at top speed across the car park.

'I didn't know you cared!' Nick giggled, and he held me tight against his chest. He smelled of sweat and beer and cigarettes and I fought against his arms. He let go and I pushed myself as far away from him as I could.

'You just keep your hands to yourself,' I snapped.

'Friendly sort of bird, aren't you?' he said.

'Leave off, Nick — she's only a kid.'

'Watch out, Kev!' someone shouted, and the car swerved at the last moment away from the 'Pay and Display' machine.

We bumped out of the car park over the pavement edge, and roared away up the Thornbridge Road.

'Soon have you home now, eh?' shouted the driver, flicking on the headlights.

'Do you have to drive so fast?' I had to shout to make myself heard.

'He always drives like this,' said the girl with spiky hair. 'He's crazy. If you think this is fast, wait till he's in a hurry!'

As if he wanted to prove her point, Kev put his foot

down and the car rocketed down the road, the tyres screeching on the bends. I gripped the seat in front, fervently wishing I'd stayed in Parr. Now it was too late, I could think of half a dozen other things I could have done. I could have taken a taxi. I could have rung my mother and asked her to come and pick me up. I could have found the police station. I realized now how stupid I'd been, to ride in a car with this crowd. We'd be lucky to get home alive!

Fortunately, there wasn't much traffic about at this time of night, only an old van a long way in front, going the same way as us. I don't know what speed we were doing but we soon caught it up. Going up a steep hill the van went slower and slower. It wasn't going fast enough for Kev. He flashed his lights a couple of times, then pulled out to overtake. We got to the top of the hill side by side – and there was another set of headlights coming straight for us.

The other girls screamed, I don't know whether I did or not. Nick shouted, 'Kev!'

Kev shoved his foot to the boards and the car shot forward – I saw his face in the oncoming headlights – he was as white as his shirt – and then swerved in front of the van just as the other car skimmed past us.

'Stop the car!' I shouted. I don't ever remember being so frightened. 'Stop – please! I want to get out!'

'So what's the hurry – we're OK, aren't we?' Kev snapped.

'I think I'm going to be sick!' That was a lie, but I had to make him stop somehow.

He sighed heavily and pulled in to the left. Nick swung back the door and I got out of there as fast as I could.

'Go on – don't wait for me,' I said, as Kev showed signs of hanging about. I held my stomach, pretending to feel ill.

'How will you get home?' asked the spiky girl.

'I'll ring my mother. I'll be all right.'

And as the door slammed shut and the car roared away down the road, I leant trembling with relief against somebody's garden wall.

The yellow street lighting showed up a deserted road. A lot of the houses were already in darkness, and some with only the bedrooms lit up. Somebody was watching a late movie, I could see the pale flicker of the TV set through the window.

I realized that I hadn't the foggiest idea of where I was. I took a deep breath and began to walk.

CHAPTER ELEVEN

What an idiot I was. And come to think of it, I'd been an idiot all along about this concert. I'd wanted to go, and I'd done it. But what good had it been? I'd enjoyed the music – some of it – but I hadn't even managed to say two words to my dad. And seeing Caroline there hadn't helped.

The incredible thing was, my mother had known what it would be like – that's why she hadn't wanted me to go. She'd tried to warn me, but I wouldn't listen. And now I was in a strange place, on my own in the dark at half past twelve in the morning, looking for a phone box – and the whole rotten mess was my own fault.

A car passed me, driving quite slowly, going towards Parr. I drew back into the shadows of someone's gateway – I didn't want any more offers of lifts from people I didn't know. The red rear lights disappeared and I walked on again.

I began to wish I'd worn my sandals. There was a blister coming on my toe, and both heels were rubbing too. This whole thing was turning into a nightmare. Didn't they have any phone-boxes in this rotten place?

A couple came out of a house, noisily shouting goodnight to a woman who stood in the doorway. They got into their car and drove away. The woman went inside and shut the door. Somewhere, a dog barked.

Just then I thought I couldn't possibly be any more miserable, but I was wrong. It started to rain, a gentle drizzle that soon settled into a steady downpour. My jacket didn't have a hood and rain soon ran in rivers off my hair and trickled down my back. The rain quickly soaked through my jacket into my dress. I hunched my damp shoulders, screwed up my eyes against the driving rain and trailed miserably on. I was limping now, and every step was an effort.

Some car headlights stabbed through the downpour and I shrunk back against the wall. The car was going slowly, and I was sure it was the same one that had passed me earlier, going the other way.

I peered at the number plate as it passed, then started to run forward, waving my arms like a windmill. It was Jonathan's dad's car. The stop lights came on further down the road – he'd seen me! And, as he backed the car towards me, I realized that I was crying with relief, the tears streaming from my eyes and mixing with the rain on my face.

I sat on his front seat and sobbed. He leaned across me and slammed the door shut.

'Thank God I've found you,' he said. 'Are you OK?' But I couldn't speak.

Every bit of me was wet. Rain dripped off the hem of my dress and made puddles that soaked into his carpet.

'Come on – let's get you home. Ten minutes, and we'll be there. A hot bath and a good night's sleep is what you need.'

I wondered why he had been out looking for me, instead of my mother.

'Your poor mother's sitting by the telephone biting her nails. She didn't know what to think when you weren't on the last bus. She was sure you'd gone back to Leeds with your father. She's been trying to get through to him, but when I left he still wasn't home. Why didn't you let her know when you'd missed the bus?'

I wiped my eyes and blew my nose and told him what had happened. He whistled when he heard about the crowd of kids I'd had a lift from.

'I'd have thought you had more sense than that. You could all have been killed!'

'I know. I should never have gone there in the first place.' I didn't mind *him* knowing how I felt. Somehow, I always felt comfortable talking to him.

'Why did you?'

'Mostly because of the music, I suppose. And I wanted to see Dad on the stage.'

'Your mother says she told you you couldn't go to the concert.'

I nodded slowly. I'd had the same feeling that you get when people put bossy notices up. 'Keep Out' nailed on a gate makes you want to go in – you'd never have thought of it if it hadn't been for the notice. And 'Wet Paint' makes you want to touch it to see if it really *is* wet.

'Being told I couldn't go made me want to go even more,' I said. 'Once I got there, I found out she was right, though, and I sort of wished I hadn't gone. I didn't enjoy it as much as I thought I would. And I never meant to miss the bus, but I lost all track of time.'

'It wasn't very fair of you to involve us in all this, was it, Sandie? Your mother thought that because you'd been at our house for tea, we must have known all about it.'

I hadn't thought of that. 'I'm sorry,' I told him, 'I really am.'

'I'll believe you – thousands wouldn't. But I'm hoping we can trust you not to be such a wally in future.' I gave him a watery smile.

Lights were on all over the house when we got back – and Bill was there too. I could have done without *him*. Jonathan's dad came in with me and told my mother about how he'd found me.

'She'd had a bit of a frightening experience,' he said, and told her how I'd got a lift, and how I came to be walking home on my own.

I expected her to go bananas, but she just put her arms around me and held me tight, in spite of the fact that I was dripping wet – she'd never done that before – then she rubbed my hair with a towel and ran me a hot bath.

'You spoil that girl, Louise,' I heard Bill say to her when I was halfway up the stairs. I stood still and listened. They say that eavesdroppers never hear anything good about themselves, and it's true.

'I'm just glad she's all right,' my mother said.

'But you told her not to go to that concert – and she still went in spite of that. And did it in such a sly, sneaky way, too! She obviously has no intention of ever doing as she's told. She's rude and cunning and deceitful, and she'll trample all over you to get what she wants. She's just like her father.'

I gasped as if someone had tipped ice cubes down my back and sat down suddenly. I'd always known I was like my father, but I'd only ever thought of it being the music bit. Was I like him in other ways too?

He didn't mind hurting people . . . no, that wasn't it. It just never occurred to him that people might be hurt by the way he acted. Was I like that?

Bill went on. 'And what was he thinking of – giving Sandie a ticket for that kind of thing? The man's an idiot!'

'He *doesn't* think – that's his trouble,' my mother said. 'I don't suppose he meant her to go there alone – but he might have known *I* wouldn't go with her. He couldn't have known she'd take off like that all by herself.'

'It's time you read her the riot act. Just look at the time – it's five past one in the morning. You've been worrying about her for hours now. And has she apologized? No, she hasn't.'

'You can't tell me anything about Sandie that I haven't seen for myself,' my mother said. 'I've wanted to slap her for some of the things she's said to me.'

'It's a pity you didn't.'

My mother took no notice of that. 'Bill – I don't think she's half as bad as she seems. She's just mixed up. This kind of thing is just part of growing up. She'll get over it, you'll see. Just give her time. She's never had any real security, and I want to give her a good home life. She'll settle down.'

'I don't want her to settle down. Not here, with us.' I could hear the squeak of his leather shoes as he walked up and down the kitchen. His voice got louder. 'You can say what you like – she's selfish and unfeeling. Look at the way she ran off to her father the other day without saying anything. You had to trek all the way to Leeds because of her that time. Are you going to keep brushing off things like that by saying she'll get over it?'

'But she *will*. I was a girl myself, you know.'

'Not a girl like that young madam.'

'Leave it, Bill. I'm tired. We'll talk about it some other time.'

'Isn't that like a woman! That's typical!' he shouted. 'As soon as she knows she's losing an argument she says she's tired! Well, *I'm* tired too. I'm tired of playing second fiddle to a kid who couldn't care less – about you or anybody else!'

'Don't shout, Bill. Everyone in the street will hear you!'

'Let them. We're going to get this thing about Sandie settled right now.'

'What do you mean, *settled* ?'

'You know very well what I mean, Louise. We had a lot going for us, you and me. We were looking forward to a good future together.'

'Aren't we still looking forward to that?'

'What kind of married life will we have with *her* in the house?'

He said it as if he was talking about a cockroach.

'Look, Louise, it's obvious to anybody that she just can't wait to get away from here. Why force her to stay when she'd rather be somewhere else? You've done your duty. You took her when her grandmother was ill. Now, send her back.'

'Mrs Harland is still in hospital.'

'Then what about your ex-husband? She's his daughter – it's time he did something for her.'

'She's my daughter, too, and I want her to stay.'

Bill strode into the hall and took his coat down from the hanger. His voice was suddenly cool and polite. 'Very well, Louise, if that's what you want. Only you can count me out. Keep the girl here. But

86

when you get hurt, don't say I didn't warn you!'

He flung the front door open and in the sudden draught my mother's silk scarf blew off the hall table. He turned to pick it up, and saw me sitting miserably on the stairs. He knew I'd heard – I could see it in his face. He hesitated, as if he was going to say something, then changed his mind and went out, shutting the door firmly behind him.

CHAPTER TWELVE

I sat there on the stairs for a long time. I felt numb inside, like the way your mouth feels when the dentist fills a tooth. Yesterday I would have hated Bill for saying all those rotten things about me.

The trouble was, most of it was true. And how can you hate somebody for telling the truth? I wouldn't have wrecked their marriage though, he ought to have known that. Because as soon as Gran was well enough, I'd be going back.

There was no movement from downstairs – my mother was being very quiet. After a bit I got up and went back down.

She was sitting on the couch, crying. Imagine crying over *Bill*! But I sat down by her side and we put our arms around each other and cried together.

'I'm sorry, Mum,' I said.

She wiped her eyes. 'You never called me that before.'

'I know.'

It was a gorgeous day after all that rain and wind the night before. The sun was streaming in through the gap in the curtains (I wasn't exactly *afraid* of the dark – not like when I was a kid and daren't get out of bed in the night to go to the bathroom in case something reached out from under the bed and grabbed me by the ankle — it was just that I felt better when I could see a bit). I'd been sleeping on my back with my arms behind my head. They were stiff and when I started to move I got pins and needles in both arms at once.

I sat up, rubbing life back into them, and wondering why my mother had let me sleep so late — my clock told me it was five past ten. What about school? And then I remembered about yesterday, and I felt the misery of it all wash over me and settle, like a chunk of ice, in the middle of my chest. It had been a rotten day — and knowing that my rotten day was my own fault made it worse.

Bill had been right: I was a pig.

But *why* was I such a pig? Sometimes I wished there was something I could do about the way I acted. Other times I couldn't care less, not even when there were rows about it. Right now was one of the first times, and I curled up inside at the very thought of how horrible I had been. Because this row was different. This time Bill had walked out on my mother because of me. I felt as if I'd ruined her life. Of course, I couldn't see what she saw in him, but I knew that to her he was something really special. She loved him, and because of me, he'd ditched her. It was all my fault. If only I'd been a different kind of person . . .

Just at that moment I'd have done anything to get him back for her, but I couldn't think of a single thing. Except to go away and never come back, and I couldn't do that. Not yet, anyway. I sighed. Why did life have to be so complicated? Bill wanted me to go. My mother wanted me to stay. And that was incredible, after everything that had happened — but I knew she meant it, and a part of me had wanted to stay, too. We'd cried together, and she'd put her arms around me – that's what mothers were supposed to be like. And what did I *really* want to do? Stay with her? Go back to Gran? I supposed I *ought* to go back to Gran as soon as I could, then Bill would come back. I didn't know what I wanted any more.

If only I could belong to a straightforward, ordinary family, like other people, with grandparents you visited every Sunday, and most of all with a dad who looked after us and came home every day at six. Not Bill, of course, but somebody who loved me for myself and really cared about what happened to me. I remembered what Jonathan's mother had said about being born into God's family, and I wondered how it happened. Perhaps I should pray. I'd never prayed in my life, only at those Harvest Festivals with Gran (not that there was anything *wrong* with Harvest Festivals, but the whole thing hadn't meant much to me at the time). We prayed in Assembly at school of course – but you couldn't call that praying. We used to nudge each other and giggle and whisper. We couldn't wait for the Head to say 'Amen'.

Real praying must be different, I thought. Jonathan said it was talking to God, just you and him. But how would I know that he was listening? I mean, he has a lot of other people to think about as well as me, some of them really important people. What if Billy Graham, or the Archbishop of Canterbury, were praying too, right now? Surely God would listen to his friends before me? But I thought I'd try it anyway.

But how did you start? What did you say? Did you have to kneel down?

I thought I'd better be on the safe side, so I got out

of bed and knelt on the floor. Now what? I cleared my throat.

'Dear God (did that sound too much like writing a letter?). I really would like to be in a family. You see, there's only my mother here, she and my dad got divorced – but I suppose you already know about that. You probably know that Jonathan's mum told me that I might be able to be in *your* family now. I'd really like that.

'I don't want Bill for a father. I love my own dad – but you can't depend on him, so I'd like you to be my father as well. Mrs Miles says you never change like people do. Could you please show me how all this happens?'

I ran out of inspiration. I got up, then remembered to say 'Amen' just so that God would know I'd finished.

Now what? I sat on the edge of the bed waiting for something to happen, but nothing did. I felt just the same. Mrs Miles had said that being born all over again was something that happened inside you, that made you part of God's family. But how did you make it happen? And when it did, did you feel any different? If only I had a book with it all written down.

And then I remembered the Bible Jonathan's mum had given me. I hadn't read any of it yet. I'd just put it away in my bedside cabinet and forgotten about it. I pulled it out. There was a piece of paper sticking out of it, right in the middle of the book. It said, 'Read Psalm 91, Sandie, and look at verse 4!' So I did.

I always thought the Bible was full of old-fashioned words like 'thee' and 'thou'. But this one wasn't like that. It even had a picture on the front. There was a rainbow and some people with their arms in the air.

And the book was full of little cartoons.

The paper was in the right page. I read the whole psalm all the way through — verse 4 was the one about being under God's wings. When I got to the end I found I'd been holding my breath. I understood most of it, and it was lovely.

It was all about God looking after his own people, keeping them safe from danger and deadly diseases, and how they were safe under his wings. One bit said, 'When they call to me, I will answer them.' I liked that — it was just as if God was talking to me — telling me he was listening after all, and that I was just as important to him as anyone else.

I sat very still, with the book open on my knee. And as I began to read it through again, the words of the psalm began to fit themselves around a melody in my head, until the music and the words slotted into place and ran together. The song swelled up inside me until I felt that my chest would burst with the pain of it, and I longed for a piano more than ever before. Impatiently I snatched up my guitar and began to play, gently picking the strings until the song took shape. Softly, I sang the words:

> 'You're my God — I trust in you,
> I am safe beneath your wings.
> I'm not afraid any more,
> Now no evil can come in.
> You are my Father and you care.
> Because I've called to you you'll answer me.
> When I'm in trouble you'll be with me,
> You are the Lord my God — my God.

As I sang I felt the icy weight in my chest melting

away until I felt warm all over − as if someone had covered me with a soft blanket. And I knew suddenly that God loved me with a special kind of love. A bit like a dad, only even more special than that.

I sang my song again, and the love filled me and swept right over me. A lump came into my throat and I couldn't sing any more.

'Thank you,' I whispered.

CHAPTER THIRTEEN

'You must be in a good mood this morning.'

My mother had slept late too – she was still in her dressing-gown. Her eyes were swollen and puffy from crying, and her hair was all anyhow, like a witch's hair. She looked as though she hadn't slept at all.

'What do you mean?' I said.

'Playing the guitar before breakfast. I'm glad *somebody* can feel cheerful.'

'I wasn't playing it because I felt cheerful,' I began, then stopped. How could I tell her how I felt inside? I knew she couldn't possibly understand. Instead I said, 'What about school? I've overslept again.'

'I'm not surprised – it must have been nearly two by the time you got to bed. You needed the extra sleep. Anyway, you can go to school this afternoon. I don't know about you, but I feel worn out.'

She looked it, too, and it was my fault. If only I could turn back the clock and make things right again! If only there was something I could do – anything – to get Bill back for her.

'What are you going to do about Bill?' I asked her.

She drew in a sharp breath, as if someone had trodden on her toe. 'There's not much I *can* do, is there?'

'Tell him I'm not going to be here for much longer.

Tell him I'm going back to Gran's. That's all he went away for – because of me. *Please* tell him. If he knows I'm not staying, he'll come back.'

My mother snorted. 'Plead with Bill Nelson? No way! He chose to break off our engagement, and that's that.' In some ways, my mother is as stubborn as I am. 'Besides,' she went on, 'there's no telling how long you'll stay here. I know your Gran's getting on, but it's still early days yet.'

It was always 'early days'. Everybody always said that when they talked about Gran. But she was getting better all the time. It couldn't be much longer now.

I put my guitar back in its old place, leaning against the wall, and thumped my pillow into shape again. 'Aren't you going down to the shop?' I asked her.

'The shop can manage without me for a few hours. That's what I pay assistants for. I'll look in for a while later on. We'll have a lazy morning for a change.'

She went off then to have her shower, and I went downstairs in my dressing-gown to put some coffee on. Once I started moving around, I realized just how stiff I was. It must have been all that walking in the rain. I ached in muscles I didn't even know I had! Still, I thought, pouring cornflakes into a bowl, I deserved a lot worse than stiff joints. I'd been a proper wally last night!

My mother thought so too.

I poured her a cup of coffee. 'Would you like some cereal?'

She shook her head, frowning, and absent-mindedly picked a few dried-up flower heads from around the Busy Lizzie plant on the window-sill.

'Listen, Sandie,' she said at last. 'About last night.'

Now I'm for it, I thought. Just as I was beginning to think she wasn't going to say anything about it . . .

'No – I'm *not* going to go on at you. You know you were wrong to go to that concert when I'd said you couldn't go. It was blatant disobedience – but you did apologize, so I'm not going to say anything else about it. What bothers me is you accepting a lift from strangers.'

I stared hard at a little round puddle of spilt coffee on the breakfast bar, squirming inside because I knew everything she was going to say, and I knew she would be right.

Just half an hour ago I'd felt good. Warm and kind and full of love, and now I felt as though my mother had pulled out a plug somewhere, and the good feeling was draining away and leaving behind my old stubborn piggish self. She was spoiling everything for me again.

To show her I wasn't listening, I picked up a teaspoon and stirred the puddle round and round, then streaked it out on the worktop into a star pattern. I hoped it would annoy her into snapping at me and changing the subject, but it didn't.

'Why didn't you take a taxi, Sandie? Or telephone? You could have phoned, and I would have come to fetch you. You know that.'

I shrugged a shoulder. 'I did think of it, but not until it was too late.'

'Jonathan's father told me those people had been drinking.'

I concentrated on the pattern I was making. My mother's patience suddenly gave out and she snatched the spoon out of my hand and sent it clattering into the sink.

'They'd been *drinking*. And you got into a car with them! *Anything* could have happened. You're an idiot, Sandie, and you deserved far worse than you got. You were very lucky.'

I was very lucky. Well, so what? Nothing *had* happened, had it? I was all right . . .

She was glaring at me but I was staring out of the window.

'I want you to promise me you'll never be so foolish again. That you'll never take a lift from anyone you don't know.'

I sighed heavily. I didn't intend to anyway. There was no need for all this 'Never go with strangers' stuff. As if I was six years old.

'Promise me.'

'All *right*! Leave me alone, for Pete's sake!'

It sounded ruder than I'd meant it to, but I wasn't going to say I was sorry. I didn't hear her leave the room, but after a minute the vacuum cleaner went on in the lounge.

I sighed again – this time a proper one. What was the matter with me? Last night my mother and I had seemed closer than we'd ever been. And this morning I'd prayed and felt close to God too. But none of it had lasted. I had blamed my mother, but I knew it wasn't her fault. She was only warning me for my own good.

I shuddered, thinking of horrible spotty Nick, and how I had to sit on his knee. My stomach churned even now, remembering the way he'd smelled of beer and sweat when the lurching car had thrown me into his arms. It suddenly occurred to me to be glad that there were some things my mother didn't know about last night!

The telephone rang, out in the hall. I left it for my mother – the calls were usually for her anyway. It would probably be the shop. On and on it rang, and I suddenly realized she still had the vacuum cleaner running. You couldn't hear a thing when you were using it – it made a noise like Concorde taking off. So I answered the phone myself.

It was Bill, and I was glad.

'Can I speak to your mother, Sandie?' he said. 'I rang her at the shop and they told me she hadn't come in yet.'

'Hang on – I'll get her.'

I poked my head around the door into the lounge. My mother looked up and switched off the cleaner.

'It's Bill,' I said, grinning, 'and he wants to speak to you!'

Her face lit up and I hugged myself gleefully as she went out to the phone. Now they'd get back together. Everything would be all right. I followed her out into the hall.

'Yes – I'd forgotten about it,' she was saying. 'It's in the cupboard under the stairs . . . Of course it's convenient, you know that, Bill. There was no need to ring me to ask that. Pick it up tonight if you like . . . All right. I'll see you later, then.'

She put the receiver down slowly, like a robot. 'He left his tool-kit here after he put up some shelves in the kitchen,' she said with a sigh. 'He's coming to call for it tonight.'

He was coming to pick up a tool-kit. Casanova with a screwdriver! So much for him wanting to patch things up, I thought grimly, scribbling savagely on the telephone pad. I might have known!

There had to be something I could do to help.

Perhaps I should find out where he lived and go and talk to him myself? Or ring him up? Surely he'd listen if I explained to him that I'd soon be going back to Gran's? There was no need for him to call off the wedding when I wasn't going to be here for much longer!

I'd do it. I made my mind up – I didn't know if it would make any difference, but I had to have a go.

I was glad when it was time for school. There was a crowd of kids around the gate, as usual, and Jonathan was sitting on the wall, swinging his legs.

'You got here at last,' he said, with a grin so wide it showed his chipped tooth. He'd got that trying to do fancy stunts on his bike. He didn't like people to know that, but he'd told me. 'I didn't think you'd be coming this morning, so I didn't bother calling for you.'

So he knew about last night. I'd been hoping his dad wouldn't have told him. I sniffed, and turned my head away.

We walked up the school driveway together and he looked at me and shook his head. 'How do you do it?' he said.

'Do what?'

'Think of such awful things to do? I'd never dare . . . You're a real dumbo, aren't you?'

I was getting fed up of being told how stupid I was, especially when I knew it anyway. 'Your dad had no business telling you about it. It's nothing to do with you, so just keep your long nose to yourself!'

He didn't say anything to that. Jonathan's one of those exasperating people you can't pick a fight with.

'I bet your mother flipped her lid,' he said after a bit.

'No, she didn't, if you must know, clever-clogs.'

I suddenly remembered about Bill, and I didn't want to talk about it any more. What would he say if he knew my mother's boyfriend had ditched her because of me?

There were some girls in front of us, from my class. I shouted, 'Kim! Laurie – wait for me!' And, leaving Jonathan behind, I ran on to join them.

'Where were you this morning?'

'Lucky you, missing games. Miss Carroll said we needed some extra exercise, and she had us doing a cross-country run. I ask you – *cross-country* in this weather! We were *melting*!'

'Weren't you feeling well?'

I shook my head. 'I hardly slept last night, and I didn't wake up till ten o'clock.'

'It's a good thing you're back, anyway. Mrs Richards sent for you at lunch-time and we had to tell her you were away.'

'What did she want me for?' My words were drowned by the bell which went just as we were walking by it. It wasn't a nice steady buzz, like at my last school. This one was like a fire-bell. You couldn't miss it wherever you were.

A horde of third-formers rushed past us down the stairs. If he'd seen them, Mr Allen would have given them a million lines. Nobody was supposed to run anywhere in the school. Especially not on the stairs.

'What for?' I yelled in Laurie's ear. 'What did she send for me for?'

'We're having a sponsored event next weekend. They announced it this morning,' she yelled back. 'It's something to do with that. Come on – we're going to be late.'

The bell stopped, and we raced down the corridor. Mr Barker – we all called him Doggy, of course – was already at his desk and we were the last ones in. There was a stupid rule that said we were supposed to be in our places before the bell stopped. It was hard luck for people without watches – but the school didn't care about little things like that. Doggy glared at us over the top of his glasses, which were half-way down his nose as usual. So, we were thirty seconds late, I thought, glaring back at him. Big deal.

'What kind of sponsored event?' I hissed at Laurie.

Doggy rapped on his desk with a ruler. 'If I'm not interrupting anything, ladies,' he said sarcastically, 'perhaps I may be allowed to teach a history class.'

Kim said under her breath, 'That's quite all right, Mr Barker.' She always talks to the teachers like that.

Doggy went on and on as usual. I felt like nodding off. Just before the bell went there was a tap on the door and a third-former came in. Doggy looked up with a sigh, and said, 'Now what?'

The girl said something to him, and he said, 'Oh, I suppose so.'

He rapped on his desk again. 'Sandie Harland,' he said. 'The pleasure of your company is requested by Mrs Richards. In the music room. I suppose that as it's the end of the lesson in five minutes, I can let you go.'

So she really had wanted to see me – and it must be something special. Well, whatever it was, I was going to find out. I followed the girl out of the door.

'And don't forget your homework,' Doggy added as I shut it behind me.

CHAPTER FOURTEEN

'Just look at it!'

My eyes followed Mrs Richards' pointing finger. 'It' was the school tape recorder. A tape recorder that must have sailed with Noah in the ark.

'I'm not going to put up with that old thing any longer,' she said determinedly, tossing back her dark hair. 'It's about time our music department had some decent equipment to work with – this lot ought to be in the museum! I've kept on about it to the Head, but it seems that we're right at the end of the queue. There just isn't any cash to spare!'

I wondered where all this was leading. She went on.

'Now, my sixth-formers came up with a brilliant idea a few days ago on how to raise some funds. They suggested that we have a sponsored school concert next weekend – a two-day concert.'

A concert lasting two whole days? I'd never heard of such a thing. But it sounded interesting. 'It's a good idea,' I replied.

She smiled. 'The Head thinks so too, I'm glad to say! I thought we'd do it like this: we'll get all the musical pupils throughout the school to perform for, say, half an hour at a time all through the day, starting with the first-years, and the fifth and sixth forms will work on until ten o'clock on Saturday night. The concert will start again at ten o'clock on Sunday morning.'

'But how will it earn money for us?'

'We can do that in two ways. Parents and friends will be able to buy tickets for the concert. They can come and go as they like during the two days' performance. At the same time, we're asking those who won't be able to come, to sponsor the ones who'll be playing.' She beamed across at me.

I was catching some of her excitement. 'How many people are going to be in it?'

'I'm not sure yet, but we're lucky at this school – plenty of people play instruments. I asked around this morning, and I had a very good response. Some of them are really keen. Susan Grainger, for instance. And Alison Perry – she plays the cello very well. And Gareth Mason says he'll play his clarinet. And, Sandie, I hope you'll play the piano for us.'

'Of *course* I will, Mrs Richards.' I was looking forward to it already. I'd have to write and tell Dad – I was wishing he lived a bit nearer so that he could come and hear me play.

'Will your mother agree, do you think?'

My mother. Of course, that was the snag. She'd die rather than see me play the piano on the stage, but I wasn't going to tell Mrs Richards that. I said, 'Oh, yes, I think she will. After all, it's for a good cause.'

I'd said it airily enough, but I knew there was no way I could tell my mother about it – she'd throw fifty different fits. But whatever it took, I meant to play in that concert.

In all the excitement of the morning I'd completely forgotten that I had decided to talk to Bill about my mother.

But as I unlocked the front door after school that

103

afternoon, the first thing I saw was his tool-kit, standing ready for him by the hall table. He'd be coming for it tonight. And if I didn't do something about it quickly, the visit would be a quick 'Hello, thank you very much, goodbye'. And that would be the end of the Great Romance.

I hated the whole idea of talking to him. I never had known what to talk to Bill about, and we hadn't exactly got off to a flying start. But I knew I had to try, even if he shouted me down. And if he did – *so what?*, I told myself grimly, trying to scrape together some courage. It wouldn't be the first time.

Slowly, I hung my jacket on a hook and picked up the telephone index. It flipped open at the right page: *'Nelson, Bill'* and it gave two numbers, home and work.

It was ten past four. No point in trying to ring him at home – he'd still be at his office. I dialled the second number, my heart beating uncomfortably fast.

A bright female voice answered straight away. 'Good afternoon. Revell Technical Services – can I help you?'

'Can I . . . can I speak to Bill Nelson, please,' I said. My voice felt shaky – I hope it didn't *sound* that way.

The girl said, 'Who's calling, please?'

'This is Sandie Harland.'

'One moment. I'll put you through.'

I almost panicked and put the phone down. What was I going to say to him? How would I begin? I ought to have worked it all out beforehand . . . I took a breath to tell the girl not to bother, and then it was too late. Bill's astonished voice came on the line.

'Hello? *Sandie?*'

'Yes . . . It's me,' I said lamely.

'Well now – what can I do for you? Is everything all right?'

'Yes. Well, no. No, it's not all right. Look, Bill, I have to talk to you. It's about my mother.'

'Does she know about this?' His voice had a sudden sharp edge to it.

'Of course not! Do you really think she'd get me to ring you up? I'll be in for yet another row if she finds out – but I've got to talk to you anyway. It's important.'

'It had better be. Look, Sandie – we can't talk on the phone. Perhaps I could leave the office early and meet you somewhere. Would that be all right?'

'Fine. Where shall I see you?'

He hesitated for a minute and then said, 'There's that hamburger place in the High Street.'

'The Burger Bar?'

'That's it. It'll only take you a few minutes to walk down there. Give me half an hour to finish up here and drive across, all right?'

'Yes.'

'See you later, then.'

The line went dead, and I stood holding the receiver like someone in a dream. Well, I'd done it. I'd actually arranged to meet him. So far, so good. But what next? What in the world could I say to him? My mind played around with a few opening sentences:

'Bill – my mother's future happiness depends entirely on you.'

'My mother is utterly devastated by your decision to call off the wedding.'

'What could I possibly say to make you change your mind?'

But nothing sounded right. It was worse than writing those rotten five-minute talks we have to do at school.

I sighed. I hoped that when I saw him I'd think of something to say.

Before I left the house I filled the kettle, peeled some potatoes so that my mother wouldn't grumble so much at my being out when she came home, and scribbled a hasty note – 'Back soon'. I'd worry about explanations later.

When I got to the Burger Bar, Bill was already there, sitting in a quiet corner at the back of the cafe.

He glanced up as I slid into the bench seat opposite him, and his grey eyes met mine. He didn't say it, but the look he gave me plainly said, 'This had better be good.'

He ordered a Coke and a coffee, while I sat there fiddling nervously with a squashy red sauce bottle shaped like a tomato.

'All right,' he said at last. 'What's all this about? You said it was important. Is your mother all right?'

'That's just it. She's *not* all right. I mean – you can't really expect her to be, can you?'

His ears were a dead giveaway. They started to go pink as usual. He was getting mad already.

'Now, look here, Sandie,' he said. 'You're interfering in things you couldn't possibly understand. Things that don't concern you. If you think that . . .'

'What do you mean, "things that don't concern me"?' I broke in indignantly. 'Of course it concerns me. This whole row is about me, isn't it? And, anyway, I'm not interfering. I've got something to tell you, that's all.'

He put his elbows on the table and looked at me over

the top of his glasses. 'Go on, then,' he said. 'I'm listening.'

I took a deep breath. 'You don't have to call off the wedding. Not because of me. I know you don't like me (well, he didn't, did he?), but I won't be here long enough for that to make any difference to you and my mother. My gran's getting better all the time. I'll be going back to her soon.'

'But your mother doesn't want you to go back there at all – you know that, don't you? She wants us to get married as planned and for you to live with us here.'

'I know,' I said miserably. 'But I can't do that.'

'Why not? I know you two never got along very well – but your mother's tried so hard to make it work this time. She was determined to make a good home for you.'

'I know. It's not that.'

'What is it, then?'

'It's my music!' I burst out. 'She simply doesn't understand. She doesn't want me to play – she won't hear of me having lessons. That's what most of the rows have been about! My dad hurt her a lot – and I remind her of him. She's afraid that if I become a musician I'll turn out like him. But I won't. I couldn't, because I'm *not* him. I'm *me*! Sandie Harland. And music's part of me. I don't feel I can live without playing, and that's something my mother can't understand.'

'I'd no idea you felt like that, Sandie.'

'Yes, well – we haven't exactly had much chance to talk, have we?'

'It *has* been rather like one long slanging match.' Was I imagining things – or was there really a hint of a twinkle in his eyes?

I said, 'I'm sorry. I've been a bit of a pig.' And it was easier to say than I'd ever thought.

'Yes, you have. But it's probably as much my fault as yours.'

I took a sip of Coke. 'So what about the wedding?' I asked him. 'What are you going to do?'

'Have you thought that your mother might not *want* to marry me? After all, I did say a lot of hurtful things. The damage is done. But I apologize for hurting *you*, Sandie. I said a lot of things I shouldn't have said. I wouldn't blame your mother if she never wanted to see me again.'

'But she does,' I told him. 'That's why I had to talk to you. I had to do something to try to make things right! I can't bear to see her looking so miserable, all because of me. That's why I'd rather go back to Gran's than spoil her whole life.'

'And I thought you couldn't care twopence for anybody but yourself! Look, Sandie – I can't promise anything – but at least I'll talk to her. And without shouting, this time. Will that do for you?'

I sat back in my seat and grinned at him. Now his eyes were definitely twinkling, and for the first time I stopped wondering what my mother could possibly see in him.

Bill glanced at his watch and gave a low whistle. 'Come on – drink up. Your mother's going to be worried about you – again. It's high time you stopped taking off without telling anybody what you're planning.'

I knew it was – but I'd been making my own decisions for a long time now. Gran and Gramps had never worried too much about where I went, as long as I was back at a reasonable time. I had a lot of freedom to do what I wanted, but when I really thought about it, I could see that my mother's way was the best. I'd been thinking she was picking on me all the time because she didn't love me and she didn't care. Now I could see that it was because she *did* care.

Bill said, 'What about it?'

'I'll try.'

But even as I said the words, guilt stabbed at me again.

What about the school concert? I knew full well that my mother wouldn't hear of me playing on stage – yet I was planning to do it anyway. Should I tell her after all? No – I couldn't. I *had* to be a part of it. And, anyway, Mrs Richards was counting on me.

But I promised myself that this would be the very last time.

'Just let me get this concert over,' I thought, 'and I'll never go behind her back again. Not ever.'

CHAPTER FIFTEEN

I made sure that I was over at Jonathan's when Bill came round that evening, so that he and my mother could have some time together. When I went back home at nine o'clock my mother hugged me. She was looking happier than she'd looked for a while, so I figured the wedding plans were back on again. I was dying to ask her about it, but I didn't. I knew she'd tell me when she was ready.

On Monday morning the sponsor forms for the concert were given out at school. I carried mine around all day, then tore it into shreds and threw it into the rubbish bin outside Macey's shop on my way home.

'I need to be in school at the weekend,' I told my mother. 'Saturday and Sunday afternoons.'

'Oh, Sandie, I wish you'd mentioned it before. It's going to be very awkward. You need new shoes and I was going to take you shopping on Saturday afternoon.'

'My old ones will last another week,' I said. 'It's not as if they let water in. They're just a bit scruffy, that's all.'

'What's so important that you have to go to school over the weekend? I'd have thought that you spent enough time there. Is it a netball match? I thought you'd dropped out of the team.'

'I have. It's not netball. It's a sponsored event.'

I rummaged through my schoolbag so that I didn't

have to look at her. My Gran always knows when I'm telling lies. Perhaps I blush, or look guilty or something. So I never told many when I lived with her and Gramps.

'It's a sponsored record-play,' I told my mother, my face still in the bag. My heart was beating fast. 'It's so we can buy some new equipment for the music department. Mrs Richards is always complaining about that old tape recorder we have to use. It makes the school choir sound like a dog-fight. We're starting the concert on Saturday morning and playing music all day Saturday and Sunday.'

'But do *you* have to be there?'

'Someone has to change the records.'

'A school with a thousand pupils – and *you* have to change the records! Really, Sandie, you do make me cross. You might have asked me before you told them you'd do it. How much am I supposed to donate to this concert? Where's your sponsor form?'

'I lost it. So you don't have to give anything.'

She shrugged. 'You know best, I suppose. But just don't get involved in this kind of thing again without asking me.'

'I won't. Sorry, Mother.'

I really was, too. But why couldn't my mother be like everybody else? Why couldn't she be at the concert, sitting in the front row like Alison Perry's mother?

Alison had bragged all week about how many tickets she'd sold, and how many of her uncles, aunts and cousins would be there to hear her play the cello, and that her mother and father were coming early on Saturday morning so that they could get seats on the front row where they'd have a good view.

'Who are you bringing?' she asked me.

'Nobody,' I told her, and I hated having to admit it. 'My dad lives in Yorkshire, and so do my grandparents. Of course, my mother would love to come, but she's going to be tied up at the shop.'

'*All weekend?*'

I nodded. 'She'd give anything to be able to come, but it's hard work when you have to run your own business. It's not just selling dresses, you know. She has to go to fashion shows and do the buying, and organize everything.'

There. I'd done it again. I'd told lies with a perfectly straight face and Alison Perry had believed me, the same way my mother had. My heart was thumping a bit louder than usual, but she couldn't hear that, could she?

I didn't like doing it, all the same. I could think of about fifty different ways that my mother could find out about the concert. I lay in bed every night that week worrying – going through every one of them in detail.

At first it was Jonathan, who came to the door to ask her to sign his sponsor form – even the pupils who weren't going to be in it were asked to support the others. Then I imagined my mother emptying the waste-paper bin out in the back garden, and Jonathan's mother hanging out nappies on the clothes line, and saying, 'How nice that your Sandie is playing in the concert.' I came out in a sweat all over when I thought of that one, because it was perfectly possible.

After that I imagined Mrs Richards – or even the Head – ringing up to thank her for allowing me to take part . . . Or my mother would bump into one of the other mothers in the street, or one of them would go into the dress shop. I'd be glad when it was all over.

I wished I could tell her the truth. It was impossible,

of course, but still . . . I knew that Christians weren't supposed to tell lies, and I remembered that prayer I'd prayed about God being my father.

I still wanted that, but it seemed to be taking him a long time to answer. It was probably because of how bad I was, I thought – and I seemed to be getting worse instead of better. I supposed God didn't want people like me in his family.

Knowing that didn't stop me telling lies, though. After Alison had believed what I told her about my mother, I said the same thing to everybody who asked.

Jonathan didn't ask. I think he knew all the time that I hadn't even told my mother about the concert. But he didn't say anything to me about it, not a single word.

I just hoped he wouldn't say anything to anybody else, either.

CHAPTER SIXTEEN

I'd hidden my music under the holly bush by the front gate, wrapped up well inside a couple of plastic bags to stop it getting damp. I did it on Friday afternoon, before my mother came home from work.

She took me into Parr for the new shoes on Saturday morning, instead of waiting another week. I would have enjoyed it any other day, but today I was in a fever in case we didn't get back in time – I was due on stage at two.

As well as the shoes my mother got me a new swimming costume and bought me some foam bath and talc, and a perfumed deodorant stick for under my arms. Sometimes my mother can be really nice. And today she was in a specially good mood – I noticed she was wearing her engagement ring again.

She said we'd eat out somewhere and I liked that idea. Gran and Gramps never eat out. Gramps says nobody in the world can cook like Gran, but I think the real reason is, they can't afford it. I was hoping we'd go to the Victoria so I could tell Jonathan about it. From Grantham Square you can look through the windows and see just enough to make you want to see more. Crystal chandeliers and whole forests of ferns and potted palms, and tables with crispy white tablecloths.

We didn't go to the Victoria. We went to Brady's instead and had cheeseburgers and french fries, and huge knickerbocker glories that made my mother worry about her figure. I'm sure it *tasted* just as good as at the Victoria, though, which is all that really matters.

In the end, I only just made it to the concert. It felt funny, being in school on a Saturday. Michael Cavendish was on the stage, playing French songs on his accordion. He was dressed in a black and white striped sweater and a black beret and had a little moustache painted on. He looked a real dumbo. I wondered whose idea that was. He was the one before me. He had half an hour to play. Playing the accordion is such hard work and he already looked as if his left arm was aching, squeezing the heavy box in and out.

Mrs Richards ran up to me when I walked in. She was beginning to despair, wondering whether my mother had changed her mind at the last minute. I didn't tell her anything at all. I'd told enough lies about this concert. All I wanted to do was to get the whole thing over without my mother finding out about it.

The fourth-year toilets had been made into a ladies' changing room for the weekend. Someone had brought chairs in and a full-length mirror, which was leaning against the wall.

Susan Grainger was standing in front of it examining the spots on her face. She wasn't on until after me, but she was a bag of nerves already.

'I wonder if they'll be noticeable from the audience,' she said.

'What?'

'My spots.'

Her spotty face was so much a part of her that I'd never thought of her worrying about them. She always laughed when the other kids called her names, but if you ask me, she was putting it on. It must be horrible. I decided that I wasn't going to laugh at her any more.

I said, 'Oh, I shouldn't think anyone will notice. They're there to listen to the music, not look for spots.'

Even telling her that didn't seem to help, though, because she was worried about the music as well. She was playing the flute, and wasn't sure if she knew enough tunes to get her through half an hour. I told her that when she got to the end of the book she should just start at the beginning and go through it all again. That made her feel better, I think.

Mrs Richards came in, looking for me.

'Michael's just finishing,' she said. 'We're nearly ready for you.'

'Do I look all right?'

'You look fine,' she said. 'Just run a comb through your hair.'

I looked at myself in the long mirror. I looked OK. No — I looked good. I had on one of my new skirts. It was navy blue, and I was wearing a lemon-coloured baggy cotton blouse with it. My hair looked nice, too, in its new style. I never used to care what I looked like, but I had changed. Perhaps I really was growing up at last.

There was a burst of applause from the audience and I knew Michael had finished. I grabbed my pile of music.

'Aren't you nervous?' asked Susan. 'Lucky you! I'm shaking like a jelly.'

The only thing I was nervous about was my mother finding out about it, but I couldn't explain that to Susan. I didn't say anything.

I passed Michael coming down the steps at the side of the stage. His face was tomato-coloured and his painted-on moustache was running in the heat. He was wiping beads of sweat off his forehead, and he looked thankful to have finished.

'Good luck,' he whispered.

'Merci, monsieur,' I said pointedly, and then wished I hadn't, because he whipped off the beret, and his cheeks turned an even darker shade of scarlet.

The grand piano had been moved to almost the centre of the stage. It was a long time since I had played to an audience. People at school had listened to me practising at breaktime, of course, but this was different. I hadn't had time to be nervous before, but suddenly all I could think of was all the people in the hall, sitting there, watching me. Listening for any mistakes I might make.

My fingers felt stiff, and I fumbled for the chords. I knew 'Für Elise' backwards. I could have played it in my sleep – only today I couldn't play it at all. I felt my cheeks getting hot and I knew my ears and the back of my neck must be bright red. I knew people must be saying, 'Poor thing – she can't have been learning for very long.'

I looked up when I finished the piece. Mrs Richards was signalling to me from the side of the stage. 'Relax!' she said in a loud stage-whisper.

I began to play Schubert's 'Serenade', and before long I found I was relaxing without having to think about it. I was playing the music for its own sake, caught up in its beauty, and I had forgotten all about the people out there and what they might be thinking about me. I played on and on. Beethoven's 'Moonlight' and the 'Pathétique'; 'Clair de Lune' and a Chopin Nocturne.

People came and went. At least, they came in. I

didn't see many of them go. At last I changed from classical music to one of my own compositions. I had never played it for anyone else, not even for Mrs Richards. But today seemed the right time.

I played in a way I had never played before. Now my fingers were picking out brand new chords that hadn't been there when I wrote it – but the sound was beautiful, like the ripple of the sea, gently stirring the pebbles on the shore. Then the music changed. I could feel the storm. It was in my fingers – a flash of sudden lightning. A menacing rumble of thunder in the distance. Wind-swept, white-topped waves rolling together and crashing on to the beach. You could hear it all in the chords I was playing.

There wasn't a sound from the audience. Unless I looked to make sure they were still there, I might have thought they'd all crept out and gone home, and left me completely alone, playing to an empty school. Then, suddenly, a baby started to cry somewhere, and the spell was broken.

I looked out across the heads of the people – and I saw Bill, sitting in the shadows at the side of the hall. Next to him was my mother.

I knew I had stopped playing, but there didn't seem to be any way to make my fingers move again. There was a rushing sound in my ears and I felt suddenly very sick, and light-headed at the same time. I felt myself slipping sideways, and the piano keyboard came up to meet my forehead – I heard the horrible jangling sound it made – and the next thing I knew, I was on the floor with a lot of people bending over me. I heard Mrs Richards say, 'Give her some air,' and somebody undid the top button of my blouse.

I'd never fainted before in my whole life. It was just

my luck to do it on a stage in front of a hall full of people! I felt so embarrassed I could have died. The Head himself carried me into the girls' room – I remember vaguely wondering if he'd ever been in there before.

He sat me on a chair and pushed my head down between my knees.

'You'll feel better soon.'

I recognized my mother's voice and shut my eyes and groaned. I would never feel better. I'd let her down again and now she'd really hate me. Someone pushed a cup of hot sweet tea into my hand. I can't stand tea, but I gulped it down, anyway, and my head cleared a bit.

'Can I have a word with you, Mrs Harland?' I looked up and saw Mrs Richards steering my mother out through the doorway.

I stood up. There was a bump on my head the size of an egg where I'd hit the piano, and my legs were wobbly, but I could walk.

'Are you all right, Sandie?' That was Alison Perry. I hadn't seen her come in.

'Do be careful, Sandie. Where are you going?'

'I'm OK,' I snarled, then recognized Susan Grainger. 'What in the world are *you* doing here? Shouldn't you be playing your flute?'

'They're having a fifteen-minute interval. Look – don't you think you should sit still for a while?'

'Mind your own business.'

I picked my jacket off its hook and walked out of the girls' room, down the corridor and out of the school. I found I was walking faster and faster, my legs getting stronger all the time.

I went straight to Jonathan's house.

He was sitting in the middle of the floor, building towers out of wooden bricks, so that Splodge could knock them down again. He took one look at me.

'She found out, didn't she?' he said.

I'd been right all along. He *had* known about it. I sank into a chair. My legs were trembling again.

'Did *you* tell her?' If he had, I'd kill him.

'Course not. What do you take me for?'

'Then how did she know? I'd like to know how she found out.'

'I've no idea.'

We sat in silence for a bit, then Jonathan said, 'Was it awful?'

'Yes, it was awful. I saw her and Bill sitting in the audience, and I fainted on stage – that's how awful it was.'

'I meant, was it awful when she found out? What did she say to you?'

'What did she say?' I echoed his words. I was twisting my fingers around a button on my jacket pocket, twisting and tugging at it. It came off in my hand and I stared down at it stupidly.

'Nothing, yet.' I could hardly get the words out.

If only I'd told her in the first place! How was I going to face her, after this? . . . And Bill, too. After all he had said to me that day in the Burger Bar. I felt like dying.

The door opened, and Mrs Miles came in, manoeuvring a heavily-laden shopper-on-wheels over the threshold. She was surprised to see me.

'Why, Sandie!' she said. 'Aren't you supposed to be at the school concert? I'm sorry we missed your playing this afternoon – I had the shopping to do. But we're all going to come tomorrow.'

I said, 'I won't be playing tomorrow.'

'Her mother found out about it,' Jonathan told her. 'She turned up at the concert with Bill, and Sandie fainted.'

'I should have told her,' I said in a low voice. 'I knew all along that I should have told her. But if I had, she wouldn't have let me play!' I was close to tears.

Mrs Miles came across and sat on the arm of the chair I was sitting on. I hid my face in the sleeve of her coat and she put her arm around my shoulder.

'Poor Sandie!' she said sympathetically. 'You're always in some fix or other! How do you feel now?'

'Ashamed,' I whispered. 'I feel ashamed.'

CHAPTER SEVENTEEN

I told Mrs Miles everything. How I'd told my mother we were having a sponsored record-play. How I'd told all the kids at school that she'd give anything to come to the concert.

I said, 'I never used to tell lies like that. Well, not often, anyway. Nowadays I'm not just *bad*, I'm getting worse! After this, I *know* my mother won't want me any more. My dad doesn't want me, and neither does Bill – and God doesn't want me, either!' I was feeling very sorry for myself.

'What do you mean? Of course God wants you!'

Well, I might have known she'd say that. But how did she know? She didn't know me like God did. After all, people only know what they can see, and you try to make sure they don't find out the worst things about you. But God is supposed to be everywhere at once. He can see all the rotten bits that other people miss. I *mean*, he can even read your mind!

'How do you know he wants me?' I asked her.

'What makes you think he doesn't?'

'How *can* he want me? What have I ever done for him? Nothing. I'm not even a nice kind of person. And besides – I once prayed about it. You know – after you told me about being in God's family. But I didn't feel any different afterwards. I don't even know how you can tell when God answers a prayer like that! I mean,

122

with some prayers you'd know right away – say, if you asked God to help you pass an exam, and you did. But this kind of praying is different.'

'Listen to this, Sandie,' she said. ' "I will never turn away anyone who comes to me." Jesus said that. He won't turn away *anybody* who wants to be part of his family – whatever they've done, whatever sort of person they are!'

'What – the bad people as well?'

'Especially the bad people. None of us is perfect and we all need God's forgiveness – and his help. Have you asked him to help you?'

Of course I hadn't. I'd been thinking he wouldn't want me at all, because of all the rotten things I'd done lately! I wish I'd asked her about it before.

'But I did pray about it – and I didn't feel any different,' I said.

'Well, pray again,' she told me. 'And this time, believe what Jesus says. He loves you, and he wants you. And if you're really sorry, then he's always ready to forgive you. You might feel different straight away – but you might not. That might come later. Don't believe what you *feel* – believe what God *says*.'

I really wished I could. But how would being a Christian make any difference? My mother would still be the same – and so would Bill.

Mrs Miles said, 'You're feeling really mixed up about everything, aren't you, Sandie?'

I suppose I was. I stared glumly at Jonathan's old school photo in a frame on the mantelpiece. It had been taken when he was a little boy, and he looked really goofy. He had two front teeth missing, and he must have just had his hair cut. It was all flat on top of his head – he looked like a friendly version of

Frankenstein's monster. It had been taken a long time ago, before everything had been turned topsy-turvy. Long before I came here . . .

I sighed and said, 'It wasn't like this when I lived with Gran and Gramps.'

'I know. But nothing ever stays the same – only God, of course! Life changes, and you have to change too. And sometimes you won't like it because it means having a mother who doesn't want you to play music. Or having a stepfather like Bill that you don't get on with.'

I remembered talking to him in that Burger Bar. He'd seemed quite nice then. Perhaps, after all, he wouldn't be all that bad as a stepfather.

Mrs Miles smiled and squeezed my hand. 'Problems don't often go away,' she said, 'but if you're a Christian you can face up to them in a different way. Because you and God are working together to sort things out.'

Maybe she was right. Maybe I'd give it a try.

But before that, I had to go home and face my mother and Bill. How had they found out about the concert? My mother hadn't known this morning, I was sure. She would have said something about it. What would happen now? She wouldn't just let it pass – not this time. Perhaps she'd stop me going over to play the piano at Jonathan's. And make me come home for lunch, so I couldn't play at school either.

Mrs Miles must have known how I was feeling, because she said, 'Would you like me to go home with you?'

I shook my head. 'No, thanks – I'll be all right. After all – they can't eat me!' And I gave a short laugh.

It might have sounded brave, but it was just a put-on. My stomach felt as if it was tied in knots, and there was a horrible fluttering in the pit of my stomach that wouldn't go away.

I got a shock when I walked into the lounge. Our headmaster, Mr Millard, was there, talking to my mother and Bill and looking very much at home in the big easy chair, a cup of coffee in his hand. Mother and Bill had their backs to me, but Mr Millard was facing me. I stood stock still in the doorway.

'Thought I'd look in and see how you were,' he said to me. 'That was a nasty turn you had. Very nasty. Must have been the heat, I suppose. I noticed young Cavendish mopping his brow a couple of times. Feeling better now, are you?'

'Yes, thank you, sir.' I bit my bottom lip and stared down at his size eleven brogues, stuck out in front of him like big brown canal barges.

'Come in and sit down, Sandie,' said my mother gently, patting the place next to her.

With my head down I crept in and sat down. I didn't dare look at my mother. I wondered how much she had told Mr Millard. I knew they'd been talking about me behind my back . . .

Mr Millard said, 'We've been talking about you, Sandie.'

He must be a mind-reader. I bet a million pounds I know what they've been saying, too. No more music, I thought to myself.

He went on. 'I've been telling your mother about the annual Music Festival in Parr. It's held every November — the school usually has a few entrants, but we've never taken the trophy. Judging by today's concert, though, our standard has gone up by leaps and bounds. You'll have to start practising for it right away.'

I said, 'What, *me?*'

'Of course, you. We can't let all that talent go to waste, can we, Mrs Harland?'

My mother said, 'No', and I couldn't believe I was hearing right.

'Mrs Richards will have to begin coaching you right away – your mother tells me she's still looking around for a good tutor for you.'

I just lost a million pounds.

I looked at my mother for the first time, and our eyes met. It was amazing. She wasn't cross at all! She smiled at me. 'Your playing was beautiful, Sandie,' she said softly. 'Mr Millard is right. We mustn't let all that talent go to waste.'

'Thanks, Mum,' I whispered. I didn't want to die after all.

'How come?' I asked my mother. 'How come you changed your mind? And after I'd told such awful lies about the concert!' I couldn't understand it. There were so many questions I wanted to ask.

Mr Millard had driven off back to school, where the concert was still going on. I was sitting in an easy chair sipping hot chocolate which Mum had insisted on making for me – as if I was an invalid!

'How did you find out about it?' I went on. 'I *wanted* to tell you – honestly. But I thought that you'd never let me be in it.'

She and Bill held hands and looked into each other's eyes – real mushy, hearts-and-flowers stuff. I wonder if anybody'll ever look at me like that?

126

After a long time my mother said, 'Will you tell her, or shall I?'

I wished *somebody* would.

Bill said, 'We didn't find out about the concert until after you'd gone out this afternoon, Sandie. You didn't see the poster in the newsagent's window, did you? Very decorative, it was. Announcing the concert and listing all the people who were going to play in it. You were about half-way down the list!'

A poster! That must have been the only thing I'd never thought of!

'We only called in there to buy a paper, so we carried on walking – down to the school to hear you play!'

I looked at my mother and said in a low voice, 'But you've never *wanted* to hear me play. You told Mrs Richards you'd never allow me to be a musician!'

'You've got Bill to thank for that,' she said. 'He told me how you went to talk to him about me the other day – and if I'd known about it at the time I'd have curled up and died! I ought to box your ears. You've got a real cheek, Sandie Harland! But luckily for you, it turned out to be the best thing you could have done!'

'Why?'

She smiled to herself. 'Bill came to see me that night, and we had a long talk. About us, and about you – we talked about everything. He told me what you'd said, and he made me understand how you felt about music.'

'I told her there wasn't much chance of you turning out like your dad,' Bill chipped in. 'I used to think so – but you made me change my mind.'

'I'm sorry, Sandie,' my mum said. 'I'd never let myself look at it from your point of view!'

'I'm sorry, too,' I whispered.

It seemed as if God was beginning to sort things out

for me. I knew I still needed time to sort things out with him. Perhaps I hadn't been giving him much of a chance, before. I began to feel happy inside.

But what about the future? There were so many things to think about. So many questions still in my mind. What was going to happen when Gran was better? Should I go back to her and Gramps – or stay here with my mum and Bill? Would I ever be part of a *real* family, like Jonathan and Splodge?

I didn't know. But, as Jonathan's mum says, nothing ever stays the same – only God, of course. As for the three of us – Mum, Bill and me – things were changing – for the better.

'Well,' said my mother, 'I suppose the first thing we'd better do is find you a music teacher.'

'And a piano,' said Bill.